'Nice body.'

'Yes,' Bart agreed. 'He's my best stallion.'

'I didn't mean the horse,' Alessandra replied honestly, smiling at the man's surprised look. 'You're in good shape. Do you work out regularly?'

He climbed over the fence to stand six inches above her five feet six.

'If you mean in a gym, then no. I reckon I get enough exercise working this place,' Bart told her.

Alessandra smiled. 'I reckon you must at that!'

Dear Reader

Spring is here at last—a time for new beginnings and time, perhaps, finally to start putting all those New Year's resolutions into action! Whatever your plans, don't forget to look out this month for a wonderful selection of romances from the exotic Amazon, Australia, the Americas and enchanting Italy. Our resolution remains, as always, to bring you the best in romance from around the world!

The Editor

Alison Kelly, a self-confessed sports junkie, plays netball, volleyball and touch football, and lives in Australia's Hunter Valley. She has three children and the type of husband women tell their daughters don't exist in real life! He's not only a better cook than Alison, but he isn't afraid of vacuum cleaners, washing machines or supermarkets. Which is just as well, otherwise this book would have been written by a starving woman in a pigsty!

IRRESISTIBLE ATTRACTION

BY
ALISON KELLY

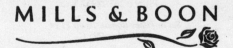

MILLS & BOON

MILLS & BOON LIMITED
ETON HOUSE, 18-24 PARADISE ROAD
RICHMOND, SURREY TW9 1SR

*First published in Great Britain in 1994
by Mills & Boon Limited*

© Alison Kelly 1994

*Australian copyright 1994   Philippine copyright 1995
This edition 1995*

ISBN 0 263 78937 3

*Set in Times Roman 10 on 11 pt
01-9504-56995 C*

Made and printed in Great Britain

CHAPTER ONE

Bart Cameron looked up from the task of grooming his favourite stallion as a pick-up was brought to a dust-flurrying halt. He'd heard it long before it came into view, and reason told him it was the woman his sister Marilyn had talked him into hiring as a bookkeeper for the summer. He wasn't thrilled at the idea of having to play host to a tourist for twelve weeks, but Bart had never been able to refuse his older sister's artful cajoling. He knew it was time to start trying, though, the instant the woman opened the vehicle's door!

He watched in silence as a slim peroxide-blonde moved towards him. Long, shapely legs stretched from what a vivid imagination might call shorts and a snug yellow T-shirt did nothing to conceal the wearer's delicate curves, nor the fact she was braless. He judged her age at around twenty-five. If this woman was as hard up for work as Marilyn had led him to believe, then it was only because Hugh Heffner's talent scouts didn't know she was in the country!

'Gidday! Can you tell me where to find Bart Cameron?'

'I'm Bart Cameron, ma'am. You must be Marilyn's friend, Alexandra.'

'*Alessandra*,' she corrected.

'Sorry, ma'am.'

'Don't worry about it; I've spent half my bloody life trying to teach people how to pronounce my name!' She laughed. 'But drop the "ma'am", uh? It's positively matronly! Hell, I'm only twenty-eight!'

5

Her voice was reminiscent of Katherine Hepburn's, if you could ignore the harsh language and broad accent.

'Alessandra. Unusual name.'

'After five boys my dad wanted something really feminine.' She gave a deep, throaty laugh. 'Unfortunately he got me!'

'I'm nearly finished here,' Bart said, indicating the horse and silently deciding that her father must be darned hard to please. 'If you don't mind waiting a few minutes until I'm through, I'll help you take your stuff into the house.'

'No rush,' Alessandra assured him, grasping the post and rail fence surrounding the corral and pushing against it as she stretched first one leg then the other behind her. Her actions drew a puzzled look from Bart Cameron.

'Just getting a few kinks out,' she explained. 'Drove without stopping for the last four hours.'

He nodded and returned his attention to the horse.

Alessandra immediately hoped she'd have a chance to ride while she was here. She loved horses almost as much as she hated office work, but, she rationalised, she had to eat. Before Bart Cameron had agreed to employ her as a bookkeeper things had looked financially grim. After twelve months backpacking round the USA she'd returned to Australia penniless.

Bart's silence as he continued grooming the stallion gave Alessandra the opportunity of assessing the man and comparing it to what Marilyn had already told her about him. She knew he'd been widowed eighteen years earlier and since had devoted himself to raising his daughter Lisa and building up his ranch in Texas. Four months ago he'd purchased this cattle station on the Queensland-New South Wales border as an experimental extension of his American ranching operation. Marilyn had said he was thirty-eight. Alessandra decided he looked nearer his mid-forties, his weathered appearance no doubt attributed to spending so much time outdoors in the harsh climate. He wasn't good-looking in the conventional sense of the word—in fact she wasn't sure she could stretch charity far enough to describe him as ruggedly handsome—but he had an honest, strong face that people would trust. His body was another matter altogether, she decided; worn denim and chambray more than hinting at male physical perfection hidden beneath. A one-time aerobics instructor, Alessandra recognised quality when she saw it; Bart Cameron's body was definitely top quality! He gave the stallion a final pat then turned quickly, catching her appreciative expression.

'Nice body,' she said, unable to suppress a sheepish grin at being caught.

'Yes,' Bart agreed. 'He's my best stallion.'

'I didn't mean the horse,' she replied honestly, smiling at the man's surprised look. 'You're in good shape. Do you work out regularly?'

He climbed over the fence to stand six inches above her five feet six.

'If you mean in a gym, then no. I reckon I get enough exercise working this place,' he told her.

Alessandra smiled. 'I reckon you must at that!'

Bart pulled his stetson lower on to his forehead as they walked to where she'd stopped the pick-up at the foot of the porch steps. This didn't seem like any bookkeeper he'd ever known! What he needed was someone to handle the financial side of things for twelve weeks, not a house guest! He had enough problems right now with Lisa, without having to ride shot-gun on the accounts as well.

'Have you had much experience with accounts work before?'

'On and off. I've worked on several occasions for my brother's building firm and I also did a stint with a film company in Greece. I've done both computer and manual processing, so I don't anticipate any difficulties here.'

'Good, because I can't spare the time to give you anything more than a basic explanation of how things operate; you'll be on your own with the books. This all the luggage you got?' he asked, holding a battered leather suitcase.

'That and this,' she replied, pulling a small backpack from the front seat. 'When you've done as much travelling as I have you learn to pack economically. 'Struth, it's hot!'

Bart made no response to her observation of the climate. He wasn't one to waste his breath making irrelevant comments or endorsing accurate ones. The woman seemed to have no such reservation.

'You're obviously used to this heat. At least it's dry heat and not that oppressive humidity you get up FNQ! Is that exhausting!'

As they reached the top of the porch stairs, Alessandra became aware of the close scrutiny of the man next to her.

'Is something wrong?'

'FNQ?' he enquired in a slow drawl, accompanied by a look that suggested he wasn't sure he wanted to hear the translation.

Alessandra laughed.

'Far North Queensland. FNQ. Sounds like an obscene way of saying "Get lost", doesn't it?'

She turned, catching the smile her reaction had caused, and was stunned by the transformation in his face. Strong white teeth were exposed from behind the previous thin line of his mouth, and deep grooves appeared at the sides. The fine lines spreading from the corners of his eyes, no doubt created by years of squinting against the sun, suddenly became laughter lines, lending a boy-like roguishness to his face. When he smiles, she thought, he is almost *more* than conventionally good-looking!

She accepted his offer of a cold drink and sat quietly in the air-conditioned comfort of the kitchen as he busied himself at the refrigerator.

All the mod cons were evident and in sparkling condition. Grey Formica benching and cedar cupboards ran the length of three walls, separated by a strategically placed stove, refrigerator, microwave and the largest domestic freezer she had ever seen! Soft grey walls complemented the black slate floor.

'Here you are.'

She turned in response to the rich Texas drawl.

'Uh . . . thanks.' She barely restrained a sigh as she accepted a glass of what was obviously lemonade and watched him pull the top off a can of beer. Oh, well, she'd suffered lemonade before and it hadn't killed her... Mind you, it wasn't likely to kill her thirst, either!

Leaning against the bench, Bart watched her take a tentative sip from the glass. He wondered what whim had possessed her to bleach her hair to stark white, or for that matter why she wore it so short. It was completely straight and cut into a bob that ended an inch below her ears with a fine fringe just tipping her eyebrows. The hair, along with the elfin chin and fine, turned-up nose, created a pixie-like look that seemed in total conflict with the sensual blue eyes, rimmed by blue-tipped lashes.

As the father of a teenage daughter, he was only too familiar with the use of mascara and kohl, but he'd never struck anyone who used *blue*! Why would anyone want to have blue eyelashes?

'You're staring, Bart.'

The truth in her words startled him back to reality.

'Sorry, I just noticed you weren't really enjoying that drink.'

'Well, it's pretty damned hard to enjoy a *lemonade* when you're watching someone drink a frosty-cold beer!' she responded cheekily.

'Oh!' Bart felt chastised. He hadn't thought to offer beer, since none of the women he knew drank it. 'Would you prefer a beer?'

She grinned. 'Can a duck swim?'

'Sorry, I'm not used to women drinking beer. Here.'

Alessandra smiled at the speed with which he put a can on the table.

'I'll get you another glass...'

'Don't bother, a can will do me.'

She was already lifting the beer can to her mouth and a hot spark of sensation shot through him as she took two long swallows. He wondered how watching a woman do something as unladylike as guzzling beer from a can could be physically stimulating.

'Ahh!' She gave a blissful smile. 'Now that felt good enough to call orgasmic!'

Bart sent her a startled look, wondering whether some cosmic force was putting them on to the same wavelength. The notion didn't bear thinking about!

'I have to get back to work. I'll show you your room, since I'm sure you'll want to rest.'

'What I'm hanging out for is a swim. Although I'll settle for a shower.'

'I'm afraid the swim will have to wait till Lisa can show you a safe spot in the stream.' At the dejected look on her face he only just stopped himself from offering to take her there himself. He didn't have time to pander to the whims of someone who was here to work for him. 'Dinner is at seven-thirty. We don't usually dress for it unless we have guests.'

'Righto! I'll remember. Dinner in the nude at seven-thirty.'

Bart gave a wry smile as he desperately pushed away mental images of himself trying to eat a meal while a naked Alessandra MacKellar sat opposite. Already he felt the effects of heartburn.

'Listen, will you do me a favour?' she asked.

'If I can,' he said tentatively, picking up her bag to take upstairs.

'Smile more often,' she said. 'You have one helluva sexy smile, Bart Cameron!'

Bart was sure he was the only thirty-eight-year-old man ever to blush!

More tired than she'd realised, Alessandra awoke to find she had only twenty minutes until dinner. She felt sure Bart Cameron's don't-dress-for-dinner rule wasn't flexible enough to allow her the luxury of arriving at the table in a satin and lace camisole. Time to unpack.

Packing and unpacking wasn't difficult for Alessandra; in fact she could manage to make herself at home in a new place in a little over ten minutes. Rolling from the bed, she lifted her suitcase on to it and proceeded to do just that.

Her meagre wardrobe consisted mainly of jeans and trousers which she teamed with either brightly coloured T-shirts or sweatshirts, as climate dictated. There were two hand-embroidered calf-length skirts she'd bartered for in Israel and a length of colourful hand-painted silk, purchased last year in Hong Kong, should she need something more dressy. Alessandra had never been one to get overly hung up on fashion, probably due to growing up with a tribe of brothers, and her only concessions to feminine vanity were expensive underwear and a collection of gold and silver jewellery, which she'd gathered from various parts of the world over the last nine years.

The last items she pulled from her case were three brass-framed photographs, which she set on the dressing-table. One was of a smiling middle-aged couple against a backdrop of ocean. She had taken the snap four years ago when, following her father's retirement from his plumbing business, her parents had moved to the north coast of New South Wales.

The second photograph was of her five brothers—Greg, Drew, Scott, Brad and Matt. Scott and Matt were both single while the other three were married with seven children between them. The remaining snap was of the children and their mothers.

Bart waited for her as she descended the stairs.

'Settled in?'

'Yes, thanks.' She gave him a wide smile. 'It never takes me long.'

'Good. Lisa has dinner ready, so we better get in there.' He stood aside to allow her to pass, hoping she didn't have a sensitive stomach—his daughter's cooking was definitely an acquired taste!

'Wow! I *love* your hair!'

'Thanks!' Alessandra smiled pleasantly at the teenage girl, who hadn't waited for a formal introduction.

'Is it bleached?'

'Lisa!'

'Only by the sun,' Alessandra replied, ignoring Bart's apologetic expression at what he considered rudeness on his daughter's part.

'I wish I was a blonde!' Lisa Cameron sighed, pushing savagely at her waist-length dark hair.

'I dyed mine black once when I was thirteen,' Alessandra confessed, and laughed at the teenager's horrified expression. 'My parents' facial reaction was pretty much similar to yours now!'

'Dad would *kill* me if I changed mine!' she said with more than a trace of resentment.

'You've got that right,' Bart Cameron stated.

'Why?' Alessandra asked, causing both heads to swing in her direction. 'It's her hair.'

'That's what I keep telling *him*!' Lisa said.

Bart sent a controlled glare across to his most recent employee.

'Lisa is only seventeen years old,' he replied, as if that explained everything.

'Nearly eighteen!' his daughter responded.

'With luck you might make it.'

The tone of the exchange between father and daughter told Alessandra she had walked into a struggle of awakening independence versus old-fashioned discipline. The atmosphere wouldn't be dull around here, that was for sure, even if the cutlery was. Cripes! How was a person expected to cut steak with a blunt knife? She diverted her plan of attack to the creamed potatoes, only to wish she hadn't as the half-cooked vegetable caused her to gag.

'You OK?' Bart Cameron enquired, and Alessandra wasn't sure whether she imagined the hint of humour she saw in his eyes.

'Eh, sure! A bit just went down the wrong way,' she lied, now suspecting that the inability to cut the steak lay in its cooking and not the knife. 'Do you kill your own meat?' she asked, in an effort to forestall having to take another mouthful.

'Usually. The Rough Rivers Brand has the reputation of producing some of the finest beef cattle on either side of the Pacific.'

Alessandra tried to look impressed, while wishing that it hadn't lost quite so much of its reputation on the way to her plate!

'We have beef for dinner every night when the housekeeper is on vacation. It's the only thing Lisa feels confident about cooking.'

God help us if she ever tries to tackle anything else! Alessandra prayed silently as she managed to sever another piece of meat and insult her taste-buds with it.

From then on conversation was limited to enquiries about the health of Marilyn and her family, and Alessandra explained how she had met Bart's sister in California and become firm friends with the older woman and her husband and children. It was Marilyn, knowing that Alessandra was planning to return to Australia for the summer, who had suggested that she apply for the job at Rough Rivers.

When Bart began to talk to Alessandra about the ranch's accounting system, Lisa announced she had a date and excused herself from the table in the wake of a paternal instruction to be home before midnight.

Through it all Alessandra continued to try and force herself to eat; finally she gave in and pushed the plate aside. She looked across the table to find her employer leaning back in his chair watching her. His gaze caused a pool of warm liquid to settle in her lower abdomen.

'Well, that was certainly...filling,' she said. 'I couldn't eat another bite.'

'Not many people would,' Bart replied drily. 'Lisa isn't exactly overly talented in the kitchen.'

His humour was no longer only hinted at, but bursting out in a smile so dazzling that Alessandra felt almost giddy.

'Now there's an understatement! May I ask what perverse pleasure you get out of watching visitors choke on raw vegetables and charred steak?' she asked, having no intention of making polite noises about how it wasn't *that* bad.

'I figure it's about time Lisa learnt to cook...'

'At what cost? A manslaughter charge?'

'She'll get better with practice,' Bart stated.

'It would be healthier for everyone if she got better with *instruction*! Besides, cooking isn't absolutely essential to a woman's armoury these days. Wouldn't you be better off hiring a replacement while your regular housekeeper is away?'

'Lisa wouldn't make any effort at all then. Can you cook?' he asked.

'No. But I'm sure as hell better than your daughter! Which isn't to say I'm prepared to take over the task, if that's what you have in mind.'

'It wasn't,' he assured her, standing and commencing to clear the plates from the table. 'Would you care for dessert?'

'Only if it comes out of a tin.'

'What about frozen pecan pie and ice-cream? I'll even defrost the pie first,' he promised. 'Though I'm not sure Lisa would.'

Alessandra wondered whether he would use the microwave or simply conserve power by directing his denim-blue eyes on it; for a man who wasn't good-looking he certainly had some powerful extras!

'Suddenly I'm starving again! And as a dedicated, card-carrying member of the women's movement I feel obligated to enjoy having a man cook for me!'

By mutual consent they ate their dessert in the kitchen.

'What made you decide to become a rancher? Marilyn told me you both grew up in Dallas.'

'Even as a kid I always preferred country life over the city. My uncle used to let me spend every vacation on his ranch, working for him. When I was old enough to quit school I did and moved out there for good. When my uncle died he left the ranch to me. Twelve months ago I decided to take a chance and began looking around for an Australian property.' He shrugged. 'So here I am.'

'You don't regret it?' she queried, sensing the conversation would end there if she didn't.

'Why should I? Do I look as though I have regrets?' he returned, holding her vivid blue gaze. Not because he wanted to, but because it was hard not to be drawn into the peacock-blue depths of her eyes.

'No. But few people can claim to have no regrets about their lives.'

'Do you have regrets?'

Alessandra grinned, 'No! Not for the last nine years, at any rate. I can honestly say I've done everything I have ever wanted to do so far with my life, and I can't see that changing in the future. Mind you, other people have spent a great deal of time regretting things on my behalf! My girlfriends, boyfriends, lovers, brothers, parents...'

Realising this woman needed very little encouragement to talk, Bart made no comment as he began to stack the dishwasher.

'Boy! Have my parents spent some time regretting some of the things I've done. Like the time I was arrested for assaulting a police officer...'

Bart swung around, not certain he'd heard her correctly.

'For *what*?'

'For assaulting a police officer,' she repeated calmly.

'You see, I was taking part in a protest at White Bar, in Sydney, about the shipping of yellow cake...uranium,' she qualified, 'when the guy I was with was suddenly hit by a copper. I mean, Rick—that was the guy's name—wasn't doing anything worse than casting aspersions on the copper's bloodlines when—*whammo*!'

She swung a clenched fist at an imaginary figure and winced.

'The boys in blue suddenly wanted to exercise their fists on Rick's face! Well, hell, what was I supposed to do? Stand back and not even try to help him? Don't say yes, because that's exactly what the judge thought too. But I was lucky, I only got fined a couple of hundred bucks. Even though it was the second time I'd been picked up by the cops.'

'The *second* time?' Bart wondered just what sort of woman his sister had sent him!

'Yeah, but I got off with a caution the first time. That was for kicking the door on a car after it had run over my dog. They bought the plea of shock that Dad's solicitor thought up.' She smiled smugly. 'In actual fact I was mad as hell and if my brother hadn't grabbed me I'd have kicked more than the car door!'

'Um—how long ago did all this happen?' He hoped she wasn't about to say, 'Only last month.'

'I was fifteen when my dog was killed and nineteen the second time. Don't worry, I'm not a hardened crim. I'm not about to slit your throat in the night and take off with the family silver!' she teased.

If this woman claimed she had no regrets about her life to date, one thing was certain—she wasn't hard to please! He poured two cups of coffee and carried them back to the table. Already Alessandra was into a heartfelt monologue on why uranium shouldn't even be mined, let alone used for the production of nuclear weapons. He would kill Marilyn for inflicting this on him! Not only was he at the mercy of the emotions of an increasingly difficult seventeen-year-old daughter, he now had to contend with a radical feminist who would probably talk underwater with a mouthful of marbles! Suddenly he could claim one very real regret—he regretted that, on top of everything else, Alessandra MacKeller had to be sexy into the bargain!

Without a doubt this was going to be the longest summer he'd ever had to endure!

Two days later, Alessandra entered the kitchen to find the teenage Lisa eating breakfast. Except for presenting herself at dinnertime, along with her usual unappetising excuses for meals, the girl had made herself scarce.

'Good morning. Can I get you some breakfast?'

Alessandra gave a wry smile and leant against the refrigerator.

'Do I look *that* desperate to eat?' she asked the young brunette.

'Pardon?'

'Lisa, you may have your old man fooled, but don't try and come the raw prawn with me,' Alessandra told her.

'Come the ... raw prawn? I don't understand ...'

Alessandra poured herself a cup of coffee from the pot on the stove before seating herself at the table.

'It's an Aussie expression that means, "don't insult my intelligence". I know a con job when I see one.'

'I don't know what——' Lisa began.

'*No one* cooks as badly as you do without putting in a lot of effort! Even a person with absolutely no comprehension of electric appliances would show gradual improvement. Unless, of course, they were deliberately trying to sabotage the food. Your efforts are too consistently bad to be genuine.'

Alessandra watched the guilt rise in a tide of red from the girl's neck. Her hunch was right.

'Look, kid, I don't know what you're trying to prove, but if you have the idea that your father is suddenly going to give in and hire another cook, forget it. I already suggested that and he wasn't buying.'

'He wouldn't! Daddy thinks just because my mother was a terrific cook I have to be too. I never even knew my mother! But between him and Grandma I feel like I'm a clone or something!' Lisa pushed her plate aside and propped her chin on her hands.

Alessandra noted that the dark brown depths of her eyes, although sparkling with rebellion, also hinted at confusion.

'Every vacation for as long as I can remember I've been pushed into learning something that my mother learned as a girl and excelled at.' Lisa sent an assessing look at the older woman, as if trying to gauge the wisdom in discussing family matters with a stranger. Alessandra said nothing and finally the teenager continued. 'It started with ballet at four and has covered just about everything from music and art to equine sports! Their latest programme is an all-girls college! Well, I'm *not* going!' she said, flicking a waist-length plait over her shoulder. 'No matter what, I'm not going.'

Alessandra let out a soft sigh; her sympathies were definitely with Lisa. She took a thoughtful sip of her coffee as she gauged the prudence of stepping into something which clearly had nothing to do with her. Yet the memory of a long-time friend demanded she do just that. She finished her coffee and pushed the mug across to Lisa.

'Pour us both another,' she said, giving the girl a smile of understanding, 'and tell me what *you* want to do.'

'I haven't time. I have to meet someone.'

'Oh. Well, perhaps another time.' Alessandra smiled. 'I have to get cracking on the accounts at any rate.'

'I told Dad I'd show you a safe swimming hole later today. What time do you want to go?'

Alessandra sensed Lisa's edginess, but made no reference to it.

'Any time this arvo is fine with me,' she replied easily. 'Ah . . . ?'

'Any time this *afternoon*. I can see I'm going to have to remember that we're dealing with a language problem here!'

Lisa nodded. 'I'll be back about lunchtime.'

Alone, Alessandra finished her coffee. Bart Cameron would be back later to see how she was progressing with the accounts. For some reason her body churned with anticipation.

Alessandra spent the best part of nearly two hours cursing Bart Cameron's bookkeeper, as she tried to interpret the accounting procedures used in the various cash ledgers. No one could accuse the absent Edith Wilcox of being either neat or methodical! In an effort to clear her mind of the jumble of figures whizzing about, Alessandra shook her head vigorously.

'Having problems?'

Startled, she turned quickly to see Bart Cameron standing in the doorway of the tiny office. His presence seemed to reduce the room's size. She decided to credit her accelerated heart-rate to his silent unexpected appearance rather than his inherent masculinity. It was wiser.

'You surprised me. I don't like people creeping up on me.'

'I didn't "creep", but I am sorry if I startled you. You were so busy talking to yourself you obviously didn't hear me call out as I came into the house.'

'I wasn't talking to myself.' Alessandra smiled, matching his amusement. 'I was pouring out verbal criticisms of Mrs Wilcox's handwriting, as you no doubt heard.'

Bart nodded. 'I came in about the time you reached the decision that as an accountant she was, "About as useful as teats on a bull"!'

'It's true.'

'I'll take your word for it. I've never been able to make out her scribbling well enough to judge. Fortunately for me my auditors can.'

'They were probably employed as code breakers during World War II or have studied ancient hieroglyphics in Egypt.'

Trying to keep her gaze from wandering over his body, Alessandra focused on the black stetson he twirled on his finger.

Where the crown met the brim, beneath a small braid of leather, she could see the tell-tale stain of what was probably years of perspiration. Illogically, *that* rather than the time spent poring over the ranch's financial records convinced her of Bart Cameron's dedication to hard work. Blisters and sweat were something that this man knew intimately. She wondered if there was a woman alive who knew him equally intimately. If so, she envied her. *'Struth!* Where had that thought sprung from?

'You look hot. Why don't you join me for a cold drink before we carry on any further?' Bart suggested, noting her flushed face.

'Hot'! 'Carry on'! Alessandra almost choked as he said the words. The man had no idea how well he could read minds!

'Good idea!' Alessandra endorsed, moving to the doorway as if she were dying of thirst.

Bart sensed her unease and knew he had caused it. While it was true he considered Alessandra MacKellar to be more than just a little rough around the edges, he had hoped his feelings weren't obvious, having no desire to hurt her. Sighing softly, he followed her to the kitchen, determined to ignore the tantalising swing of her hips.

'It's almost lunchtime. I can fix us a couple of sandwiches, if you like,' Alessandra offered.

Bart surveyed the clock hanging on the kitchen wall. Generally he didn't eat until about one, but the idea of sharing a meal with someone appealed.

'OK. If it's no bother.'

'I'm not Lisa; I think I can handle a couple of sandwiches,' she said drily.

'I don't suppose you'd consider a trade?' Bart asked wryly as he pulled assorted jars and containers from the refrigerator.

Alessandra eyed him cautiously.

'Such as?'

'I'll make lunch if you make dinner.'

'I thought dinner was Lisa's chore.'

'It's the "chore" of anyone who has to try and eat her cooking!'

'Tell me something I don't know.'

'So you'll do it?' He looked up eagerly, sensing unspoken agreement in her tone.

'On two conditions,' Alessandra said, grinning at his raised eyebrows. 'Firstly, Lisa will continue to cook the evening meal, but under my guidance. I think you'll be quite surprised at the improvement ...'

'If there's an improvement it'll be gratitude not surprise I'll be feeling! And the second condition?'

'That you'll allow me to work as a jillaroo.'

'A *what*?'

CHAPTER TWO

'A JILLAROO. Female version of a jackaroo. You know, a stockman...a *cowhand*, or whatever you Yanks call it!'

'No way! I haven't time to baby-sit some woman while she plays at being a cowgirl. This isn't a dude ranch, Alessandra. You're here to do the accounts, not have a holiday at my expense.'

'Listen, mate! For a start, I haven't needed a baby-sitter for twenty years! Nor am I under any illusions as to just how hard it is to run a cattle station...I've done it more than once before! Heck, I've mustered everything from stray lambs in Victoria to brahmin bulls in the Northern Territory!'

Bart watched enthralled as fiery sparks lit the blue depths of her eyes. He noted the defiant jut of her chin and the steely conviction of her own belief in her abilities. His silent appraisal seemed to spur her on.

'I'm not asking to be treated like a tourist, Bart. I'm an experienced rider and used to working with cattle. At the very most the accounts will only take me about five hours a week to keep up to date...'

'There's also the payroll,' he reminded her. 'That involves driving into town to the bank and back again. A three-hour excursion in itself. Plus tallying up each hand's earnings for the week——'

'All right, take out one day for organising the wages,' Alessandra conceded. 'But that still leaves me with six days of empty hours on my hands. I'll go mad with boredom! Besides, I want to earn my keep; I hate feeling like a free-loader.'

23

Bart leaned back against the bench, folding his arms across his chest. She swallowed hard at the sight of his shirt straining against his muscular frame, shocked by the tide of sexual awareness he generated in her. No man had ever made such an instant impact on her senses.

'Well?' she asked.

'Tomorrow I'll check out your riding ability...'

She nodded. 'That's fair enough.'

'Providing,' he added with a half-grin, 'that I'm not suffering the effects of tonight's dinner!'

'Thanks for not letting on to Daddy about me deliberately ruining his meals,' Lisa said shyly.

Alessandra swam a few strokes further from the edge of the river before answering.

'Since you're so desperate to prove yourself an adult in his eyes, my telling him would only have had the opposite effect. Childish spite isn't a means by which to prove maturity.'

The pretty brunette dragged herself out of the water and draped herself in a towel.

'Nor is promiscuity,' Alessandra added knowingly.

'Uh?' The younger girl's face was a mixture of surprise and guilt.

Alessandra couldn't help the small smile of sympathy that crossed her face. She made her way to the bank in an easy breast-stroke motion.

'I know a love bite when I see one, Lisa. Or a hickey, as you say.' Instinctively the girl's hand reached to her neck. 'It's a bit late for that.'

Lisa's eyes became shiny with tears and Alessandra felt a wave of pity at the obviously confused teenager. Why was it that in every generation the teen years were always the most difficult?

'Are you going to tell my father?'

'Heck, no! The potential for blackmail would be destroyed then!' At the girl's shocked expression

Alessandra ceased teasing. 'Hey, I'm joking! Mind you, as a kid I wasn't so generous. I used to blackmail my older brothers and their girlfriends unmercifully! It was very profitable too, I might add. I scored new roller skates on one occasion from Scott and a surf-board from Brad on another—that was for keeping quiet about him throwing a party when he was supposed to be baby-sitting me.'

Alessandra smiled at the memory. She'd been a real terror as a kid and not much better as a teenager. She suspected some of her antics would send Lisa into shock and her strait-laced father into cardiac arrest! Slanting a look at the hesitant girl who stood a few feet away unsure whether to stay or leave, Alessandra had a feeling that Lisa's rebellious streak sprang from desperation rather than temperament.

'I won't tell your Dad, Lisa,' she assured her softly and saw relief flood the girl's face. 'Are you serious about this guy?'

'I don't know. I think so. I mean, Todd's the nicest guy I've ever met.'

'What does your father think of him?'

Lisa gave a bitter laugh and shrugged her shoulders.

'He doesn't approve of him, but I don't care what he thinks. It has nothing to do with him.'

Alessandra finished towelling herself off and pulled her T-shirt on over the *maillot* she wore.

'Well, if dinner is to be ready on time, we'd better get a move on back to the house.' She handed the younger girl her clothes. 'I've got a deal with your old man that I'll oversee your cooking if he agrees to let me work with the hands around the ranch.'

'You're kidding! Daddy has agreed to let you *work with the cattle*?'

'Once I prove I can tell one end of a horse from the other. What's so surprising about that?'

'My father firmly believes, "Ladies do not belong around cowhands, corrals or bars! Nor do they smoke, swear or drink beer!" And that has been quoted to me from the time I was in the cradle!' Lisa said.

Alessandra struggled to contain a grin. She could just imagine Bart Cameron saying the words.

'Lucky for me I don't smoke. Uh, Lisa?'

Bart Cameron entered the house to the sound of uncontrollable laughter coming from the kitchen. Lisa? Heck, he couldn't remember the last time he'd seen her without a surly look on her face, let alone heard her laugh.

'Of course the guy could hardly believe the fact that little old pint-sized me had tossed him over my shoulder and sat him on his ars——'

'Good evening, *ladies*.'

Both Lisa and Alessandra swung around at the heavy tone of the male voice. Alessandra noted the sudden change in Lisa's expression.

'I was just telling Lisa about the time a guy tried to pick me up on a train.'

'Yes. I heard the rather graphic description,' Bart said curtly. His tone made the younger girl cringe. 'Do I have time for a quick shower before dinner, Lisa?'

'Umm...' The girl looked at Alessandra for an answer.

'Sure, but quick is the operative word. Another ten minutes and I won't guarantee that the chicken won't be ruined!'

Bart seemed about to say something, but changed his mind and merely nodded before leaving the room.

'Well he can certainly kill a party just by his presence!' Alessandra remarked.

'He's in a bad mood,' Lisa confided. 'I can tell.'

'That's a relief, I'd hate to think he was that bloody unpleasant every evening after work! Set the table, would you, Lisa?'

A phone call interrupted the meal almost as soon as the three sat down to the table. It was for Bart, and with obvious reluctance he pushed his plate of spicy chicken aside and went to take the call. Lisa and Alessandra enjoyed a light-hearted conversation which, although it never rested on one subject for long, revealed a lot about the younger girl to Alessandra, parts of it touching a wound she'd thought long healed.

'Sorry about that,' Bart said, returning to the dining-room just as the others were finishing the last of their meals. 'Business that couldn't wait. Don't feel you have to keep me company while I eat,' he said with more generosity than he felt. He loathed eating his evening meal alone. It reminded him all too much of the lonely time immediately after Kathleen's death, before Lisa had been old enough to sit alongside the table in a highchair.

He looked across at his child's classically beautiful face and was again reminded of her mother. Kathleen had been barely four months older than Lisa was now when she'd died. For years he'd feared his daughter might have inherited not only her mother's beauty but also the asthma which claimed her young life. Fortunately Lisa had been spared that.

Alessandra was sensitive to the awkward silence drenching the atmosphere and wondered if anyone else noticed. Bart didn't appear interested in generating any small talk, and Lisa, although looking uncomfortable, seemed reluctant to move. Suspecting the teenager was anxious to discuss something with her father, Alessandra politely excused herself. Taking an apple from the fruit bowl in the kitchen, she let herself out into the warm night air.

She located a log, beneath a huge tree of indeterminable age, and sat down in the night's dark peace. Propping her elbows on her knees, she cradled her chin, looking out in the direction of the legendary Black Stump. In the blackness, all she saw was a network of twinkling lights stretching for miles. Whoever had written the song about the stars in Texas being big and bright had missed out on the magic of sitting beneath Australia's Southern Cross. *Here* the stars were bigger and brighter than anywhere in the world, including the heart of Texas!

But she frowned even as the famous tune played in her head. Actually, she was in danger of taking a particular Texan too much to heart. With no encouragement from him at all, she was more than a little interested in Mr Bart Cameron.

There was something about the man that stirred up the three years of dust which had settled on her sensuality. He, of course, didn't appear to be even remotely attracted to her, and she had to admit this was understandable, considering they had next to nothing in common. So why did he hold such an attraction for *her*?

Bart Cameron was staid and conservative to the point of being almost boring. She, on the other hand, was what her brothers described as a 'radical extrovert, who bordered on fruitcake'! So why was she so drawn to the cowboy? Maybe it was the flashes of loneliness she caught glimpses of from time to time, but, if that was the case, then surely what she was feeling hinged on pity? No, Bart Cameron created a lot of different feelings within her, but *pity* definitely wasn't one of them!

Just roll with the punches and see what happens, she told herself.

After all, she wasn't the type for coy games when it came to the opposite sex; five brothers had taught her that men preferred women who were honest about their feelings, and subtlety definitely wasn't one of her strong points.

Rising, she took a healthy bite of the apple she'd been absently polishing against the leg of her jeans, and ambled off in the direction of the corrals. Eventually her feet led her into the stables.

Only four horses were housed in the building—the stallion she'd seen Bart grooming and three others. She was instantly drawn to a magnificently proportioned chestnut.

'Well, aren't you a beauty, fella?' she whispered, reaching a steady hand towards him. The animal whinnied aggressively, taking a step backwards.

'Easy, mate. I'm not going to hurt you.' She edged nearer, aware of the uneasy brightness in the animal's eyes. 'Steady, boy... You're a beautiful fella, aren't you...hey?' Again the horse loudly protested her presence. It was as he turned sideways that Alessandra noticed he'd been gelded.

'No wonder you're angry. What sort of stupid moron wouldn't want to use you for stud purposes? Well, don't you worry, handsome...this is one female who thinks you're perfect just the way you are...'

The muscular horse raised himself on to his hind legs, exhaled a hysterical snicker, and lunged at the gate that separated them. In the blink of an eye she was forced savagely against the wall on the opposite side of the long narrow building and shaken by the forearms.

'Are you completely stupid?' Bart demanded to know.

'I will be if you keep pounding me into the bloody wall!'

The vibrations stopped; the verbal insults didn't.

'You must be the most idiotic woman I've ever met! Redskin is a maniac! You could have been killed!'

'So what are you trying to do—finish the job? Let go of my arms before I lose all circulation to my hands! *Thank you*!' she said, stunned by the effect his closeness was having on her.

He took a step back, casting a quick glance at the still restless horse before steering her by the arm away from the front of the stall.

'I didn't mean to hurt you. Are you OK?'

She shook her head.

'What's the matter?' His voice held alarm. Her eyes seemed even brighter than usual and her face was slightly flushed.

'My heart is pounding a million miles an hour.'

'It's probably due to the fright you got when Redskin reared,' he said, trying to keep his gaze from moving to her breast to check her timing.

'No. It's entirely your fault.'

'Look...' He ran a weary hand through his hair and sighed. 'I'm sorry, Alessandra, but all I was thinking about was getting you clear of the gate in case the brute crashed over it and struck you with a hoof. I acted on instinct. I'm sorry if I scared you.'

Alessandra considered what sort of a reaction she might get if she were to reach up, put her arms around his neck and kiss him. She could always plead delayed shock as an excuse if he objected to her actions.

Half an hour earlier she hadn't been convinced that Bart Cameron was 'her type'; suddenly she knew that no other man would ever come close to affecting her the way he did! Her shortness of breath wasn't the result of Redskin's antics; it was due entirely to Bart Cameron's closeness and overwhelming masculinity. Yet it was more than simply his physical presence that was making her heart expand and crowd her lungs. It was the gentleness of his concern. Yep! Here was the man for her, and all she had to do was let him in on her discovery. But a full-frontal attack somehow didn't seem the right approach. She needed to be *subtle*!

'You didn't scare me, Bart.'

'But you said——'

'I *said* you were responsible for my increased pulse-rate. I never said you *scared* me.'

'What...?'

'Night, Bart; see you in the morning!'

Turning quickly, she hurried across to the house, leaving the stunned man still standing in the stables. As

she reached the kitchen she allowed herself a little
chuckle.

'That's about as *subtle* as you can get, Alessandra
MacKellar!'

Bart was tired and irritable from a fitful night's sleep.
He wasn't in the mood for Lisa's sulking, nor
Alessandra's dry wit and inane chatter. He poured a cup
of coffee and took it outside into the early morning
sunshine.

He couldn't think of one reason why the Lord would
see fit to inflict the torment of the last two days on him.
The events of last night alone were enough to age a man
twenty years! What with Lisa announcing that she didn't
want to go back to the States to go to college and threatening to leave home, then to walk out to the barn and
find Redskin all set to trample a sassy-mouthed
Aussie...! Hell!

The easy solution was to ship Lisa off to her grandmother in Houston and then to tell Alessandra that he
didn't require her services as a bookkeeper.

Ha! His mother-in-law would like nothing better than
for him to admit he couldn't handle his own daughter!
She'd been telling him so for nearly eighteen years. He
wasn't about to prove her right now.

The Australian was another matter. She and Lisa
seemed to get on like a house on fire and he had to admit
his daughter's cooking had improved two hundred per
cent under the older woman's guidance. What bothered
him was that, while the girl's cooking was taking a turn
for the better, in the few days Alessandra had been here
Lisa's language had definitely taken a downward slide.

Last night, during the argument they'd had, Lisa's use
of expletives would have made a marine cringe! There
was also the matter of Alessandra 'coming on' to him.
Well, at least that was what he assumed she had been
doing. It didn't seem all that logical, sitting here in the

harsh light of day. After all, he was much too old for her, and with her looks she could have her pick of almost any man she wanted. Bart wondered why the idea depressed him, because she certainly wasn't his type.

Sure, she was sexy as all get out, but sex appeal went only so far; at some point femininity had to make a stand. He suspected that Alessandra equated femininity with rabies—to be avoided at all costs!

He drained the last of his coffee from the cup and headed back to the house. He wouldn't fire her... yet, but he sure as hell was going to have a few words to say about her language!

'Get a load of this!'

A shrill wolf whistle drew Bart's attention from the task of saddling his horse, and instinctively he knew who was attracting the appreciative whistles of his men, even before he looked up and saw Alessandra striding across towards them.

'Man, wouldn't I like the job of *pouring* her into them jeans every morning!'

'It's all yours Jim, s'long as I get the pleasure of peeling 'em off her every night!' came the laughing reply.

'Knock if off, fellas,' Bart warned, unusually irritated by their comments. 'The lady's working here for the summer and I don't want any trouble. Got it?'

'Hey, boss, they were only foolin' 'round,' Jim, the foreman Bart had brought with him from Texas, replied.

'And I'm just telling them the facts,' Bart said.

'Gidday!' Alessandra beamed, letting her welcome include them all. She received a mixture of responses and greetings, from everyone except Bart, who simply inclined his head and ran his eyes over her from head to foot. As a means of ignoring him she made a point of introducing herself to each of the men.

'When you're through socialising...' Bart said.

Alessandra wondered what had put him into such a
foul mood. The men returned to their work and she
moved to where Bart stood holding a saddled bay mare.

'You didn't have to saddle her; I could have done it
myself.'

'I didn't,' he said. 'Yours is over there.' He pointed
to a corral that held three horses. 'The grey. This isn't
pony club, Alessandra. You catch him, you saddle him,
and *then* we'll see if you can ride him.'

Alessandra drew herself up to her full five feet six and
gave him a hard glare.

'Easy!' she said, swinging away from him.

'Probably,' he agreed. 'The hard part will be trying
to mount him in those jeans. I imagine sitting must be
difficult.'

'Enjoying the view?' she asked sweetly, deliberately
swishing her bottom, but not turning around.

Bart would have bitten off his tongue before ad-
mitting that he was finding it almost impossible to keep
his eyes off her. Yet it was the truth. Alessandra
MacKellar was making him feel things he didn't want to
feel. Not about her anyway!

Alessandra didn't expect to have the slightest bit of
trouble catching the gelding and putting the bridle on
him. She'd spent a great deal of time with horses. Over
the years she'd gained valuable experience with many
different breeds, having worked as a strapper with
thoroughbred racehorses in Australia, Britain, Ireland
and New Zealand; while the time she'd already spent on
outback cattle stations in Australia had instilled a great
respect and admiration for the hard-working, well trained
stock horses used on the properties. She'd even had a
couple of seasons of barrel racing on the rodeo circuit.

She genuinely loved horses, which perhaps was why
the animals seemed to trust her almost instinctively. Of
course that lunatic Redskin had been an exception! Bart
admitted he was crazy, so why keep him? she wondered,

knowing all too well the risks of hanging on to a psycho horse. Well, she'd worry about that later; right now she had to prove her horsemanship to a tall, lanky hunk with a medieval view as to how a woman should behave.

Bart watched as she approached the horses with a respectful caution. He was too far away to hear the words, but he could see by the movement of her mouth that she was talking to them. He recalled the softly soothing tones he'd heard her using the previous night on Redskin. Did she use that same seductive tone when making love to a man? An electric current shot down his spine at the thought. Irritated, he clamped his hat further on to his head.

'Move your butt, Alessandra! I haven't got all day, you know!' he shouted. His angry tone sent the grey skittering out of Alessandra's reach, and she swore loudly. 'Charming language for a lady!'

Alessandra took another couple of minutes to secure the bridle to the grey and lead him back to where Bart sat perched on the fence.

'What's his name?' she demanded, deciding she wasn't going to wear his bad mood with a smile for a moment longer.

'Pewter,' he answered, lifting an expensive, hand-made saddle from the fence and handing it to her.

She took it without a word and inspected it with interest.

'Checking for burrs?' he queried smugly.

'Actually I was thinking that the thing has so much padding and is so deep that a person would have more chance of falling out of an *armchair*! An Australian stockman wouldn't use one of these as a matter of pride!'

Bart let the remark go unchallenged. It would have served her right if he'd given her one of the old worn saddles! He refused to dwell on the reason why he hadn't. He watched her go about putting the object in question on the horse. She was careful to fold the stirrup straps across the saddle before easing it on to the grey.

Silently he applauded her. It was a good habit to get into, as with a skittish horse the sudden impact of the irons swinging down and hitting it could often cause it to rear or bolt. Again she was sweet talking the animal as she tightened the girth. From the corner of his eye he noticed the men had stopped work and were watching her. He said nothing.

'OK, Pewter, darling, let's check the stirrups for length,' she said.

Taking hold of the reins in such a way that the horse was unable to turn his head and take a nibble on her *derrière*, she used her free hand to turn the stirrup iron towards her and in a fluid motion swung herself into the saddle.

'The advantages of stretch denim,' Bart murmured, and received a bored look in response.

She stood in the irons for a moment before dismounting. She lengthened one of the stirrups two notches, then walked around the horse and repeated the action with the other.

'Those stirrups are too long,' he told her.

'I'm sorry,' she replied sweetly. 'I thought you were riding the bay.'

'I am.'

'Then, since I'm riding this horse, I'll saddle him so *I'm* comfortable!' she retorted, remounting. This time she barely cleared the saddle by two inches when she stood in the irons.

Dammit! How could something as sweet and gentle-looking as she was be so darn stubborn? As for that hat she was wearing, it looked as if it had been stomped by a mule! The wide brim dipped down over her face, but, instead of being the smooth oval shape of a stetson, it was squared off and the crown lower, in keeping with those favoured by the Australian stockmen who worked for him. Around the band was a chain-like decoration, which on closer scrutiny proved to be a series of old ring pulls from beer cans linked together. If anyone ever accused Alessandra of dressing to make an impression, they could only mean a bad one!

'Is there something in particular you're looking for or are you merely trying to commit my face to memory?' she asked.

'Lisa could have lent you a hat, if you'd asked.'

'If I'd needed one I would have.' She touched a hand to the item in question. 'But this is my lucky hat. I take it everywhere I go.'

'It shows.'

His unexpected grin made her go weak, and Alessandra was sure if she'd been sitting in any saddle other than the one she was in she'd have ended up in the dirt on her backside!

'Mind if I walk him round a bit just to get the feel of him and the saddle?'

She could hardly credit that the squeaked request had come from her. In an effort to restore some calm to her body she took a deep steadying breath and motioned the horse into action.

It was ridiculous that she could affect him in this way, Bart told himself silently, still experiencing the warm stirring in his loins that the sight of her breasts straining against her shirt ignited. It wasn't as if he was starved for female companionship. Up until a few months ago he'd been involved in a lengthy and very physical relationship with a lawyer in Dallas. Bree had been everything that Alessandra wasn't. Elegant, sophisticated, highly successful in her career, but first and foremost a *lady*. Their relationship had ended when Bree took a job in New York, and Bart bought the Australian property, with no regrets on either side. The approach of his foreman drew him from his reflections.

'She's got good hands,' Jim observed.

'Yeah.'

'Rides mostly with her upper legs, though. Looks easy in the saddle.'

'She's got a good seat.'

'Me an' the boys noticed that even *before* we saw her ride!' Jim chuckled.

'Hard to miss,' Bart conceded with a grin. 'She wants to work with the stock.'

'Ah . . .' The cowhand was non-committal.

'Would you work with her?' Bart asked, not taking his eyes from Alessandra, who was now cantering the horse.

'Is she any good?'

'That's what we're about to find out,' Bart replied, pushing himself away from the fence he'd been leaning against. 'Alessandra! We're going to ride up to the Kilto paddock and see how well you can cut cattle. You ready?'

'Sure.'

'Jim, grab your horse and come with me. You might as well be in on this, since you're the one who'll have to answer to me for any mistakes she makes,' Bart told the cowboy.

'Hey, Jim!' Alessandra called to the departing man. 'Your job will be a breeze! *I don't make mistakes*!' She couldn't stifle the laughter that Bart's thin-mouthed expression created.

The only conversation was between Bart and his foreman and it centred around the movement of stock and the mending of fences. Alessandra rode behind them, admiring the view. She was glad to be back among the familiar eucalyptus and wattle landscape of Australia.

It took them almost fifteen minutes to reach their destination, a gently sloping hill about seventy yards above a herd of grazing cattle.

The scent and sound of the cattle filled Alessandra with nostalgia. She closed her eyes, threw back her head, and took a deep breath.

'You OK?'

Bart's voice came from beside her. She kept her eyes closed.

'Wonderful. In fact I feel almost orgasmic!'

'It must be the saddle!' he snapped.

Alessandra opened her eyes and looked at him. The late afternoon sun was conspiring with the brim of his hat to camouflage most of his face, but from the set of his mouth she could tell he wasn't in the mood for any back chat. Which was as good a reason as any to give him some!

'If it's the saddle, them I have only *you* to thank!'

Bart moved his mount closer and with one arm reached over and pulled her face to within an inch of his.

He muttered something which Alessandra didn't quite catch and then took her mouth in a hard kiss. 'Onslaught' was probably a better word, she thought, because as a kiss it fell a long way short of tender. Yet there was no denying the feel of his arms around her was enough to bubble her blood, or that the male roughness of his face against her own made her feel incredibly feminine. She offered no resistance and opened her lips eagerly to the demands of his probing tongue, yet before her brain could shift gears, from surprise to response, he released her.

She said nothing and, judging by the expression on Bart's face, he was in shock, but Jim's voice from among the cattle brought him out of it. He waved a hand towards the man, indicating he'd heard him, then eased his horse away from Alessandra's.

'That shouldn't have happened, but maybe now you'll realise your smart-aleck attitude is going to get you into a lot of trouble. Jim will tell you what steers he wants cut out of the herd; get to it.'

Alessandra hid a smile and was halfway down to where the cattle grazed before she stopped and turned in the saddle. Bart was still where she'd left him, and she knew it was because it gave him a good vantage-point to watch her work.

'Hey, boss!' she called, and got his attention. 'You taste great!'

CHAPTER THREE

ALESSANDRA didn't wait for a response; she flung her heels into the big grey beneath her and galloped into the herd of white-faced cattle. She'd well and truly shown him her hand, but this wasn't the time to consider her next course of action; right now it was time to prove she could muster and cut cattle as well as anyone!

'Let's get 'em, Pewter!'

Alessandra knew she was making quick work of the task she'd been set, but a lot of the credit had to go to the gelding beneath her. It was as if he could anticipate her every move. Time and time again his sure-footedness amazed her; it seemed he was capable of changing direction on a dime.

When all the nominated cattle were separated from the main bunch she eased herself back in the saddle and gave an exhausted sigh. Taking off her hat, she turned her head on to her shoulder to wipe the perspiration from her brow on the sleeves of her T-shirt. It made little difference, since that too was damp with sweat.

'That was pretty fair ridin', little lady! Where'd you learn to work cattle like that?' Jim wanted to know.

Alessandra was naturally pleased by the praise, but she felt even more pleasure as she noted the warmth in the smile that Bart sent her. Yes, she thought, if there's one thing in life I really want to experience it's Bart Cameron's lovemaking! She waited a moment for her heart to stop flipping before she answered.

'I've mustered cattle and sheep in just about every state and territory of Australia, and a person really can't help picking up a knowledge of the business if they spend enough time in the saddle. Still, I'd have to say that I learnt more from an old Aborigine stockman I met in Queensland than from everyone else put together.'

'Well, you're as good as any man I've ever seen!' Jim said, then looked at his boss and qualified the statement by adding, ''Fer your age!'

Alessandra laughed.

'We'd best be heading back,' Bart said, 'otherwise Lisa may have already cooked dinner. As from tomorrow, Jim, you've got a new hand.'

'That mean she'll be bunking down with the rest of us?' Jim asked. He was answered by a droll look from Bart. 'Just a thought,' he muttered.

Bart entered the kitchen just as Alessandra and Lisa were finishing washing up the pots and pans.

'When you're free, Alessandra, I'd like a word with you. I'll be in the office.' He turned to leave, then stopped. 'By the way, dinner was very nice, Lisa.'

'It was only the left-overs from last night,' the girl replied, puzzled.

'I know, but last night I never got a chance to compliment you. I was side-tracked by a discussion about your future education, if you recall.'

'I'm not changing my mind, Daddy,' the girl said, but with little conviction, Alessandra thought.

'Neither am I,' Bart stated. Without another word he left the room.

Lisa slumped into the closest chair. 'He simply will not listen to anything I say! I don't want to go to some fancy girls' college. In fact I don't want to go to college, period!'

'And he has other ideas?'

'Oh, both he and Grandma are full of them!'

Alessandra moved to the table and sat down.

'I thought your grandparents were dead.'

'Oh, not Daddy's mother. Grandma Weaver—my mother's mother. She's alive and well and living in Houston,' Lisa explained.

'I see. So your father and grandmother are quite close?'

Lisa sent her a horrified look.

'*Close*? Are you kidding? They drive each other crazy! The only thing they have in common is a desire to make me into a carbon copy of my mother—Grandma so that I can become the stunningly popular débutante that she'd always wanted my mother to be, and Daddy so that he can prove to Grandma that the courts did the right thing in granting him custody of me, instead of her!'

'You mean your grandmother fought your father for custody of you?' Lisa nodded. 'No wonder they dislike each other,' Alessandra mused.

'The thing is I'm sick of being piggy in the middle. Oh, Mac! What am I going to do?'

'Tough question. I agree you're entitled to make your own decisions, but you have to be sure those decisions are based on long, solid consideration,' Alessandra advised gently.

'Did you go to college?' Lisa asked.

'Yes, but I dropped out after only a year.'

'Why?'

'Oh, lots of reasons. Look, Lisa...' She paused to give herself time to decide how best to end this conversation without lying and without going into details about Jenni's death.

'An awful lot of things happened during my first year of university. Things that made me question the values and goals I'd been raised to respect. When I stood back and looked at them I realised that they weren't all they were cracked up to be.'

'Do you regret not finishing college now?' the girl asked.

Alessandra was tempted to lie, but she didn't. She lifted her head and looked squarely into Lisa's brown eyes.

'No.'

'You wanted to see me...'

Bart looked up from his work and saw a snowy-haired, blue-eyed pixie peeking around the door. God, she was beautiful! He shoved the thought aside.

'Yes. Sit down.'

Alessandra moved into the room and sat down on the chair across from Bart. She ran a hand through the short silkiness of her hair and questioned the apprehensive flutter of butterflies in the pit of her stomach.

Bart's face was unreadable, his mouth thinned in an unsmiling, non-committal line, his blue eyes thoughtful and wrinkled at the corners.

'I'll come straight to the point. I have no argument with your abilities as a bookkeeper. Edith's accounting methods aren't based on any recognised systems, but, judging from what I've seen of your efforts so far, you aren't having any difficulty interpreting them.'

Alessandra shrugged. 'I never expected to, once I became accustomed to her handwriting.'

'I was also more than impressed by the ability you showed with the cattle today...'.

'Pewter is a very well drilled horse. Thank you for not giving me a dud. I'd have really had to pull out more effort then!'

Bart didn't crack even the hint of a smile at her pseudo-modesty. Boy! Was his liver twisted about something? she thought.

'I never use a marked deck,' Bart told her coldly. 'Which is why I wanted to see you.'

Alessandra gave an exaggerated groan and rolled her eyes. 'This sounds serious.'

'I'm surprised you can recognise the fact,' he said drily. 'You seem to treat everything as one huge joke. You have a smart answer for everything.'

'I work at it. Counteracts the dumb-blonde image that being cursed with this colour hair sadly attracts!' she replied cheekily.

Bart was silent for several minutes. She knew he was doing it to prove a point, so she didn't satisfy him by commenting. Heck, she could cheerfully sit here all night looking at him! He apparently wasn't so keen on a duel of silence and surrendered first.

'I have agreed to let you work with Jim. You certainly seem capable enough and he has no objections at the moment. Today's Tuesday, on Thursday you'll be required to do the wages, so that gives you tomorrow and Friday to prove your worth as a cowhand. You'll answer only to Jim and take orders only from him or, naturally, myself. I'll have him give me a report on your progress on Saturday. Is that understood?'

Cripes! she thought; he was certainly playing the role of cattle baron to the hilt.

'Sure. That sounds fair enough. Is that all?'

Bart looked uncomfortable and began fidgeting with a pen on the desk before decisively putting it aside and folding his arms across his chest.

'No. There are two more things I want to get clear between us.'

The butterflies in her stomach turned into 747s at the hard tone in his voice.

'Firstly, while I'm grateful for the help and friendship you are providing to Lisa, I would appreciate it if you could refrain from swearing and using some of your more...shall we say "colourful" expressions in her presence. I won't tolerate it from my men and I see no reason why I should allow you to be the exception simply because you're female. Obviously you have adopted this sort of language as a result of your less than ladylike lifestyle. I realise breaking the habit is going to be difficult for you, but I insist you make the effort.'

Alessandra amazed herself just by managing to sit still, let alone keep her mouth shut! Swear? God, could she really give him an earful now! The gall of the man to assume he knew anything but the sketchiest outline of her background! Ooohhh! What she wouldn't like to do with the paperweight sitting on his desk!

'Fine.' She spoke through clenched teeth. 'You mentioned *two* other points. The second is...?'

Bart cleared his throat. He'd been prepared to let that remain unsaid, since her obviously smouldering reaction to his last words made the idea seem ridiculous. Not only that, he wasn't sure whether there was any real justification for what he intended to say. After all, it was he who had instigated the only *physical* sexual by-play between them.

Given her irreverent, teasing way of speaking, her remark about him 'tasting great' was probably nothing more than a throw-away line and not intended as the provocative encouragement he'd imagined.

'Well?' she prodded.

'Look, if I'm out of line here...' He stopped and swallowed hard. 'The truth is, I hope you didn't take that kiss earlier today the wrong way.'

'The wrong way?' she queried with a deliberately vague inflexion in her voice. Boy, was she going to make him squirm!

'Yes...you know, as if I was coming on to you or something. Because I wasn't.'

'Look, if you're worried about me screaming sexual harassment...'

'Eh...no. I'm not concerned about that... Look, what I'm trying to say is it won't happen again. Our relationship is strictly a business one.'

'Forget it; I have!' Alessandra said, standing and giving an overly bright smile. 'On my scale of one to ten it barely rated a one point five...'

'A one point five...'

'And that was only for the element of surprise! Was there anything else?' she asked, still smiling like a store mannequin.

Bart shook his head.

'Righto, then. I'll see you in the morning. Goodnight...boss.'

She forced herself to walk calmly from the room, gently closing the door behind her, while mentally she was describing Bart Cameron with every expletive she had ever heard and in the language of every country she had ever lived in.

Strictly business! *Strictly business!* Oooohh! She was so angry! With him, with herself, with just about everything!

She punched her pillow. It was typical, of course! She had a lot of luck, it was just all *bad*! It was over seven years since she'd been interested—*really* interested—in a man, and it had to be one who found her about as appealing as a case of the measles. Not only that, he'd all but said that he found her coarse and foul-mouthed. Sure, she tended to use the odd colourful adjective from time to time, but nothing which would cause even a raised eyebrow from a fellow Australian, and she had never used *that* word! Well...maybe once or twice...but never aloud.

As for the kiss, even though it *had* been the stuff of sky-rockets and rainbows, why make such a big deal out of it? She closed her eyes and willed sleep to claim her. Ha! Her head was filled with images of a thin-mouthed cowboy with eyes the colour of faded denim.

She rolled on to her side and stared out at the bright, full moon, trying to rationalise just what attracted her to Bart Cameron. He certainly wasn't the drop-dead-handsome type that caused women to swoon as they passed him in the street, although his body would invite a second look. She had to admit she found him sexy, yet in all honesty she couldn't put her finger on why. Perhaps it was simply her body protesting the last seven years of celibacy. She smiled in the darkness. The effects of sexual withdrawal? Not likely! While she'd surrendered her virginity at eighteen, she'd never been one to indulge in physical relationships simply for the sake of it. Two lovers in ten years wasn't exactly life in the fast lane.

Yet she knew that she'd find no hardship in having Bart Cameron as number three. Except for the fact that he had declared himself a non-starter! Well, at least I haven't made a fool of myself, she thought. From here on in she'd keep things as businesslike as he, but *she* hadn't been the one who'd initiated the kiss!

Over the next two weeks Alessandra settled into the routine of Rough Rivers without any major problems. Jim was impressed with both her initiative and her ability to follow orders, and told her so. The other hands were equally friendly when they found she was as capable as any man in the execution of her job. Each Thursday morning, Jim drove her into the bank where she cashed the salary cheque and then dropped her back at the house so that she could make up the pay envelopes for the men. She had suggested that it would make more sense to pay the men by cheque, since it would eliminate the need for someone to escort her to the bank.

'The boys like to get cash. Saves them the time of goin' to the bank before hitting the bar,' Jim told her.

Still, Alessandra conceded, if it weren't for the weekly trip into town she'd probably have gone stir crazy. At least it gave her the opportunity to stock up on the reading material that she devoured in copious quantities in an effort to keep Bart Cameron out of sight and out of mind. Actually she saw little of him, except at dinner and weekends, when she was careful to act coolly civil and guard her tongue.

Their arrangement regarding sharing the office worked to keep them out of one another's way. It was hers on Thursdays, Saturday mornings and if necessary Monday nights; at all other times Bart had access to it. Alessandra knew he spent most of his time in there keeping detailed records of his breeding plans, but although fascinated by the scale of his artificial insemination programme, she would have bitten off her tongue before questioning him about it. He'd probably accuse her of being sexually suggestive!

Lisa provided some company for her at the weekends, although it was usually limited to just a few hours, since the younger girl was rarely at home. Evidently although Bart didn't entirely approve of his daughter's relationship with Todd he was prepared to tolerate it as long as she was in by midnight.

'Say, Mac!'

Alessandra turned in the saddle and saw Jim riding towards her. She hoped he didn't want her to work tomorrow morning; she was exhausted. The hands were rostered to work every other Saturday, although they often helped one another out by swapping turns.

'What's up?' she asked as he reined alongside her.

'Well, I…that is, me an' a few of the boys thought…'

She was puzzled by the man's uncharacteristic shyness.

'Thought what, Jim?'

'Well, me an' the boys thought you might like to join us for a drink in town tonight. It ain't nowhere fancy, but, well, you don't seem to go out much an——'

'Apart from my weekly trips to the bank I haven't been out at all,' she replied, before turning a bright smile on the cowboy and adding, 'Thanks, I'd *love* to go!'

'You would?'

She laughed. 'It's the best offer I've had in ages! What do I wear?'

'Huh?'

'How dressed up should I get?'

'Ah.' He seemed to relax. 'Well, like I said, it ain't fancy—just a beer at the pub—but we usually tuck into some Chinese next door.'

'I get the picture. Where and when should I meet you?' she asked.

'Oh, we'll pick you up at the house 'bout seven. That OK with you?'

She nodded. 'I'll be ready.' He turned to leave. 'Oh, and Jim, thank you. I haven't exactly been inundated with social invitations; I appreciate it.'

Thirty minutes later Alessandra darted up the steps of the house, two at a time. Lisa was beginning dinner preparations, while Bart sat at the table drinking a can of beer.

'Gidday!' Her greeting included them both.

'How does steak and steamed vegetables sound?' Lisa asked.

'Fine,' she replied, pouring herself a glass of iced water. 'But don't bother cooking any for me. I'm going out.'

'You are?' Father and daughter spoke in stereo.

'Don't sound so stunned.'

'I'm not. It's just that you don't usually go out at night . . .' Lisa replied. 'At least you haven't since you've been here.'

'That's because no one asked me.'

Bart wondered who had done so now. It could only be one of his men, but which one? He took a sip of his beer. Any one of them, he thought. They all think she's the best thing since the Dallas Cowgirls!

'Well, I'd better get a move on or I'll be late,' Alessandra said, finishing her drink and turning to leave the room. At the door she stopped as a thought occurred to her. 'Oh, can I borrow a key from one of you? I don't have one.'

'I'll probably be up when you get back. I have a lot of work to do,' Bart said.

She was about to remind him that she wasn't Lisa and she had no intention of reporting to him when she came home, but something stopped her—the pure bitchy pleasure the idea of dragging him out of bed in the early hours of the morning inspired. She shrugged and left the room without a word. Even if she got home early, Alessandra was determined that she'd wait until she was sure Bart Cameron was in bed before she hammered on the door to be let in!

Bart dropped his fork when Alessandra walked into the dining-room forty-five minutes later. Fresh blue jeans hugged her body as if they'd been painted on and her feet were covered by new boots that reached to mid calf. The soft white blouse she wore moulded itself intimately to her every curve and its deep V neck would tempt the eyes of any male over the age of ten and still breathing!

'You look great,' Lisa exclaimed. 'You'll have to fight the guys off with a baseball bat!'

Bart was fairly certain that, dressed as she was, Alessandra wouldn't be safe if she armed herself with an automatic assault rifle.

'Doesn't she look great, Dad?'

He looked Alessandra squarely in the eye and wanted to tell her she wasn't going anywhere dressed like that unless it was with him, but at the last minute his brain kicked in over his libido.

'Yeah, I guess.'

'Don't overdo the flattery, Bart.'

Feeling a heel, he hurried to make amends as a car horn blasted outside. 'It's just I prefer dresses to jeans...'

'And I bet you look terrific in them too,' Alessandra said, giving him a patronising pat on the head and sending Lisa erupting into a fit of giggles. 'Well, I'm off.' She wiggled her fingers and headed for the door.

'Hey, who's your date?' Lisa called.

'*Dates*!' She winked. 'As in plural. A girl can't put her eggs all in one basket!'

Bart grunted an unintelligible response and forced his attention back to his meal. God, he hated steamed vegetables!

The television no longer held his interest and Bart checked his watch for the tenth time in as many minutes; Lisa should have been home over an hour ago. His anxious thoughts were interrupted by the noise of a vehicle stopping too rapidly on the gravel drive, as its occupant leant on the horn. He was already striding to the door when Alessandra's voice called his name with urgency.

'Bart! Bart!'

He cannoned into her at the top of the porch steps.

'What the hell's the matter?'

'I need you to help me get the guys——' she jerked a thumb over her shoulder towards the four-wheel-drive behind her '—down to the bunkhouse.'

'You're drunk!'

'Rubbish! I drank *Coke* all night! *They*——' again she motioned at the car '—are drunk.'

'Well, you smell like a brewery!'

'So would you if you'd had umpteen dozen glasses of beer spilt over you. Those guys spill nearly as much as they swallow,' she replied calmly.

They were standing toe to toe, and Alessandra couldn't help thinking how wonderful this man smelled, after being stuck in the confines of the pick-up truck, with three drunks. Come to think of it, even when he was slick with sweat and wrestling a contrary calf Bart

Cameron managed to smell wonderful to her. For a split-second she was certain he was going to kiss her again; instead he stepped away from her with what was clearly disgust.

'I don't suppose you happened to see Lisa in town?' he asked, running a weary hand around the back of his neck.

Alessandra shook her head. 'Isn't she home yet?'

'No, she isn't!' Bart said with irritation. 'And when she gets here she's going to wish she wasn't!'

'Calm down, Bart, I'm sure there's a very good explanation why she's late.'

'An "explanation" can be supplied over the phone.'

'Maybe she wasn't near a phone?'

'She was going to her girlfriend's, not Mars! The Austins have several phones.'

'Perhaps the car broke down on the way home...'

'Look, I'm not in the mood to stand here listening to you trying out hackneyed excuses for her. I have to get your drinking buddies to bed!'

Alessandra ignored his snide comment and proceeded to follow him down the stairs to the truck.

'What do you think you're doing?' he asked.

'Coming to help you.'

'Forget it! I have the feeling it would be like having ten people working *against me*.' Bart climbed in behind the steering-wheel and repositioned the slumped body of one of his men, giving himself more room. He stuck his head out of the window as the engine came to life.

'I'll be about twenty minutes. If Lisa gets in before I come back, tell her I want to see her before she goes to bed. That is if you can stay awake *that* long. You look like hell!'

The vehicle moved off before she could get out a reply, so she vented her anger by stomping into the house, slamming the kitchen door behind her.

Less than five minutes later she opened it to the missing teenager.

Lisa's face was green. If it weren't for the efforts of the tall blonde holding her up Alessandra had no doubts that Lisa would have slumped to the floor. It was this fact that prompted her to pull a chair from the table and angle it behind the girl's knees. With a total absence of grace Lisa sat down.

'She's had a bit too much to drink...' the blonde said.

Alessandra swore softly.

'I'm Angela Austin.'

'Alessandra MacKellar. How did this happen?'

'I guess someone must have spiked the punch.'

'What with? *Ether*?' Alessandra muttered, not buying the clichéd excuse, since as a teenager she'd used it on one or two occasions herself. She ran a weary hand across her brow.

'Think her Dad will be mad?' The blonde's voice was anxious.

'Heck, no! He's too busy being furious over the fact that she's a little over an hour late!' She sighed. 'Look, Angela, thanks for bringing her home. I'll take over from here. With any luck I can have her in bed before her father gets back.'

The blonde, looking relieved at the mention of Bart's absence, said a hasty goodbye and hurried to her car.

Alessandra figured she had about ten minutes at the most before Bart arrived back on the scene. She lifted Lisa's face to her.

'Lisa! Lisa, wake up.'

'Uh? Hi, Alessannnda.' The girl offered a weak smile with the slurred welcome. 'I fink I'm a bit dunk...'

'There's a lot of that going around tonight. Now listen to me, Lisa,' she said with urgency. 'Your father will be madder than a cut snake if he comes back and sees you like this.'

'He'll be angry, uh?' Lisa muttered.

'Homicidal would be closer to the mark,' Alessandra replied. 'So listen to me. I want you to stand up and I'll help you get upstairs. OK?' The girl's head rolled as she tried to nod. 'Good. Let's move.'

Although shorter than Lisa, Alessandra was surprisingly strong for her size. Speaking in a soft, encouraging tone, she offered both verbal and physical support as the younger girl staggered and stumbled her way up the wooden staircase. At the top she halted only long enough to gain a firmer hold on the teenager before manoeuvring her into the bedroom. Lisa gave an elated squeak as she spied the bed and in two drunken strides flung herself diagonally across her quilt.

The idea of Bart finding his daughter in such a state didn't bear thinking about. Moving quickly, she began to undress the practically unconscious girl.

'Kiddo, you're going to wish you were dead in the morning!'

When Lisa was safely tucked into bed, Alessandra went to the bathroom and returned with a cool damp cloth. Gently she wiped the young girl's face and neck. An ironic smile tugged at her mouth as she recalled her brother Scott doing the same thing for her after her first serious bout of experimental drinking.

She also remembered all too vividly what had happened during the night, and as the thought occurred to her she dashed back to the bathroom and returned with a plastic bowl.

'Lisa.' She shook the girl gently. 'Lisa...' She received a groaned response. 'If you feel sick during the night, use this. OK? Do you hear me? Lisa, if you want to throw up use this bowl beside the bed.'

Again the only answer was a half muttered, half growled groan. Sighing, Alessandra stood up and turned on the bedside lamp.

'Lisa.'

Alessandra jumped at the sound of Bart Cameron's voice from the door.

'Sshh,' she instructed. 'You'll wake her; she isn't feeling well.'

'Oh? What's wrong?'

Alessandra shrugged. 'Probably a virus or something.' She turned off the overhead light in the hope of discouraging him from moving further into the room and getting close enough to smell the alcohol on Lisa. He stepped back into the hall as she bodily blocked his passage and pulled the door shut behind her.

'A virus?' he mused and moved forward again forcing Alessandra back against the door.

'Well ... I mean, it might be ... I'm not a doctor, so I'm only guessing.' His nearness was causing the most chaotic disruption to her breathing. 'Ah, did you get the guys settled OK?'

'I simply tossed each one on to his bed and left.'

'Can't do anything more than let them sleep it off.' She endorsed his actions.

'Really? I thought you were an advocate of the damp-sponge treatment?'

'The damp...?' Realisation that Bart had witnessed her treatment of Lisa suddenly dawned. She swallowed hard.

'Where was she?' he demanded, still not making any movement away from her. Only inches separated their bodies.

'The Austins. Angela brought her home.'

'She wasn't at the Austins; I phoned them earlier. So don't lie to me. Where was she?'

'I have no bloody idea! And don't ever call me a liar again, Bart Cameron! You said she was going to the Austins, she came home with Angela Austin, so therefore I *assumed* she spent the evening there!'

She pushed him aside and headed towards her room with angry steps. It was the disappointment in his next words that made her turn around.

'How drunk was she, Alessandra?'

His face was shadowed with hurt and his blue eyes begged for her to deny Lisa's true condition. She couldn't do it, but nor could she bring herself to say 'paralytic'.

'She'll know about it in the morning.'

'She certainly will.'

His ominous tone chilled the room.

Sunday mornings were Alessandra's passion. She never rose before eleven and even if she woke earlier she would indulge herself by reading until then. Usually. Today she was consumed by restless energy, that, given the fact she hadn't got to bed until after two, should not have been present. Nine-thirty. She wondered if Lisa had surfaced yet. The poor kid was going to wish she'd never been born. Not only would she have to endure what would probably feel like the worst hangover this side of the Black Stump, but she was going to cop an earful from her father as well. Alessandra sighed loudly.

She'd been fortunate to have five older brothers who, by the time she'd reached her teenage years, had managed to 'break in' her parents, so that their reactions to her own youthful acts of rebellion, while not always reasonable in her own young eyes, were far more tolerant than those of her girlfriends' parents. Lisa had no one to run interference for her or to make her actions seem typical. From his daughter Bart Cameron demanded perfection with a capital 'P'. Alessandra suspected that until recently he had got it and that was what made the girl's sudden waywardness so much harder to accept.

Why was it people always expected so much more than their offspring were willing to give or even capable of giving?

Jenni's parents had been the ones who had first awakened her to this sad truth, but she'd seen many other cases since. Some realised their mistake in time; others, like Jenni's parents, never did. Not wishing to dwell on a subject that caused her pain, Alessandra got up and went to have a shower.

'Man, but she's somethin' else!' Jim enthused, holding his coffee-mug as if it were a life-support system.

Bart suspected it was, given the redness of his foreman's eyes.

'She even insisted on buying a round like everyone else. A ''shout'' she called it, not a round, but when was the last time you ever met a woman who didn't expect men to pay fer everything?'

'Reckon I might ask her to the rodeo dance,' one of the younger Australian stockmen enthused.

'How do you know I haven't already asked her?' another demanded.

'Don't matter one way or another,' came the calm response. 'She ain't blind, so I reckon she ain't likely to say yes to you.'

It seemed all the men were full of admiration for Rough Rivers' newest employee and for the past fifteen minutes had been conducting a meeting of the Alessandra MacKellar Fan Club!

So far as Bart could gauge, she could ride better than anyone on both sides of the Pacific, play poker better than any man breathing, and had every single man on his payroll in love with her and every married man wishing he was single. He got to his feet; he wasn't in the mood to listen to childish bickering between grown men.

He'd come down here to discuss the fencing he wanted done tomorrow. All he'd got was a sermon on the countless charms and ability of one Alessandra MacKellar. It was the last thing he needed to hear. He hadn't woken up in a good mood as it was; with the prospect of a scene with Lisa looming, he didn't want thoughts of Alessandra muddling up his thinking—as they'd been wont to do more and more often.

'Any truth in the rumour that she skinny dips down in the river?'

The question stopped Bart in his tracks, just outside the bunkhouse door, but he didn't wait to overhear any more. His blood-pressure couldn't take it!

'What do you think you're doing?'

Damn! She could tell from his tone he wasn't in his nice-guy mode.

'What's it look like? I'm swimming!'

'In what?'

She wondered if he'd suffered a heavy knock to the head. Perhaps after the verbal lashing he'd given to Lisa at lunch she'd come back downstairs and attacked him from behind with a blunt object.

'In a *creek*. You know—water.'

'Don't be smart, Alessandra,' he warned.

'I'm not. It just seems that way due to the lack of another intelligent life form in the area!'

'Are you naked?'

Alessandra was so stunned by the question that she found herself spluttering water before she could form a response. Actually, considering the high-voltage current his question had triggered through her body, it was a miracle she hadn't been electrocuted!

'No,' she said with a smile, then reached down to free herself from a skimpy red bikini pants she'd been wearing. 'But I am now!'

She calculated Bart's jaw hit the ground at almost precisely the same moment her knickers landed at his feet.

'Happy now?' she queried sweetly, even as she fumed at the man's unparalleled gall.

Bart wondered if at his age the sudden increase in his pulse-rate was likely to cause him to go into cardiac arrest. Not that it mattered, since his lungs were incapable of drawing in air and he was suffocating anyway.

'Well? What next?' Alessandra demanded.

'I want a word with you.'

'Sure . . . boss.'

She started to move towards the bank and Bart knew he should turn away, but she was clearly challenging him to watch her nude emergence from the water. He returned the challenge, standing silently as a hot excitement tightened his chest.

As the distance between herself and the river bank was reduced, Alessandra was starting to have doubts about the wisdom of calling his bluff. She knew it wasn't wise to tempt fate too far.

'Toss me my knickers.'

He gave her an expectant half-smile.

'*Please*, Bart?'

They landed just in front of her and drifted under the surface a little before her hand grasped the wispy material. Working herself into them was not an easy task, since she didn't want to expose more than her neck above the water. Finally she had them on. She waited, mainly for effect.

'Are you going to turn around?' she asked in a tight voice.

'No.'

'Fair enough.'

Bart thought he'd prepared himself for the effect seeing her practically naked would have on him. But he had never considered just how devastating her body would look covered by a skin-tight, saturated T-shirt!

It concealed and yet exposed every bit of her lush body in glorious detail, stopping at the top of her thighs. Although not visible, the scantily cut knickers were evident from their outline. He was helpless to do any-

thing more than run his eyes over every delicious inch
of her. She stood motionless, her breasts undulating with
each breath beneath the beige cotton, nipples standing
erotically erect.

'Disappointed?' Although she'd intended the query to
be sarcastic it had come out as a husky whisper.

Bart trapped her eyes with his. 'There's not a man
alive who could answer yes to that.'

Her body flooded with molten desire. She had never
been so physically aware of a man in her entire life, but
she wasn't about to leave herself open to another put-
down. Taking a steadying breath, she pushed her wet
hair back from her face and lifted her chin.

'Unless it's one who wears dresses. You said you
wanted to speak with me...'

'Believe me, lady, the *last* thing I want to do with you
now is talk!' Taking her by the shoulders, he hauled her
against the masculine hardness of his body, and she half
expected to hear a sizzle as her wet torso contacted with
the dry heat of his. It never entered her head to resist,
just as it would never occur to a drowning man to let
go of a life support.

The initial urgency of his kisses was matched by hers.
She opened her mouth to him, accepting the warmth of
his tongue with grateful delight for several seconds before
engaging it in a torrid, almost violent duel with her own.
His groan of excited pleasure was echoed by one from
deep within her as his hand burned a trail beneath her
wet shirt from thigh to waist and onward to close possessively around the swell of her breast. He withdrew
his tongue from her mouth to trail its tip along her jaw
and a thousand fires flamed within her even as tiny
shivers skipped along her spine. She tilted her head back
to allow him greater access to her neck, the movement
bringing her pelvis hard against his, giving further evidence of his arousal. The knowledge made her head swim
as the surrounding air became heavy with raw, hungry

passion. Alessandra grasped a handful of his hair and brought his oral attentions back to her mouth, where she was able to taste the sleek, smooth enamel of teeth.

All sense of logical thought was lost to her; one moment she was vaguely aware of thinking her legs might buckle beneath her, only to discover she was already lying beneath Bart's sensual male body.

His hands peeled the damp T-shirt over her head and, before the late afternoon breeze had a chance to chill her skin, his lips were raining heated kisses over it. Her fingers combed his hair with wilful abandon, her body trembling from his touch as time and time again he returned to the depths of her mouth to deliver his honey sweetness to her taste-buds. She wanted desperately to provide him with the same pleasure he gave so easily. She nipped at his shoulder, intending only to please him, but found she herself gaining unimaginable delights from the muscular strength she discovered. The intensity of her need stunned her. She had never known such an aching want, such a desperate need, and was dimly aware of a button exploding from the front of his shirt as she feverishly pushed it aside to taste more of his naked flesh.

Bart felt a shudder of desire rip through him as her hands slipped beneath his shirt and she arched against him, levering herself on his shoulders.

'Make love to me...'

Her breathless plea almost drove him over the edge. The wild, unbridled way she was responding to him was something he had never known with another woman. No woman had ever made him feel so male. Alessandra was a seductress straight out of every man's fantasy; she could excite with the practised perfection that every man dreamed about...

The notion had the effect of ten gallons of cold water.

Bart rolled off her and stood up. Blue eyes, clouded by passion, searched his face.

'Bart...?'

'Get dressed. You can drive the truck back to the house.'

'But...I...' Alessandra choked on the contempt she saw in his eyes.

'Get dressed!' he said again, this time picking up her towel and jeans, which lay near by, and throwing them to her.

'Bart, did I do or say something wrong?'

He gave a derisory laugh.

'I wish to God you had.'

CHAPTER FOUR

FOR the next week Alessandra took care to keep out of Bart's way as much as possible. This might have proven awkward had it not been for the fact that Bart was working equally hard to avoid her. Indeed, she might well have ended up talking to herself if it hadn't been for Lisa, who was only too grateful for someone to chat with, since *she* wasn't planning on speaking to her father ever again! At least, Alessandra thought, no one was arguing with anyone.

As she waited for the printer to run off a balance sheet of the monthly accounts, Alessandra wondered yet again what she'd done to turn Bart's passion to anger in the space of just a few seconds. She had no doubt that if Bart hadn't so abruptly called a halt to their lovemaking she *couldn't* have. She'd never responded so heatedly to a man before and it hurt to know the man in question didn't want a damned thing to do with her.

The shrill of the phone made her jump, but as she reached to pick it up it stopped, and as she was removing the report from the printer the office door was thrust open and Bart shoved his head in.

'I need to use the computer. Are you through in here?'

'Just about,' she said, deciding he could give a whole new meaning to the word curt. She deliberately took her time labelling and filing the report.

Bart mentally counted to ten in an effort to keep his pulse-rate steady. His hopes of squashing the attraction he felt for the white-haired Aussie by limiting his exposure to her had been for nothing. Seeing the way her blouse pulled across her breasts as she pushed her chair

63

clear of the desk was enough to rocket his memory back
to way they had tasted while still damp from her swim
in the creek.

'Bart.'

He gave himself a mental shake, realising he'd not
heard what had been said to him.

'Pardon?'

'I said would you please move so that I can get through
the door? The office is all yours.'

'Oh. There was no need to rush. Are you sure you're
finished?'

Alessandra eyed him strangely. If she didn't know
better she'd have accused him of smoking something
other than ordinary tobacco. He was definitely wearing
a Disneyland expression.

'Bart, are you OK? You seem kinda . . . strange.'

'Do I?'

Now he was giving her that stupidly boyish grin which
caused her insides to mush up. Don't let him suck you
in, she warned herself.

'Look, you said you wanted the computer. It's all
yours.'

'Alessan . . . oh, hell! I've left Doug Shaffer waiting
on the outside phone!' Moving past her, Bart snatched
up the receiver of the desk phone. 'Do me a favour and
hang up the kitchen extension, will you? Oh, by the way,
I'll be driving into town on Thursday, so we'll be leaving
early. Hello, Doug? Sorry to keep you . . .'

Alessandra lay in bed for a few moments, telling herself
that she was no more pleased about making the routine
trip into town for the wages with Bart than she normally
was with Jim. Bull! her inner self roared. You've just
woken up from the most X-rated dream you've ever had
and the leading man wasn't Jim! Gritting her teeth, she
willed herself not to smile—to no avail. She let loose an
excited giggle and swung herself off the mattress.

'Face it, kiddo,' she told her reflection in the mirror, 'you have the hots for Bart Cameron something fierce.'

Slipping on her old towelling robe, she was about to head for the bathroom when there was a knock on her door.

'Alessandra, may I come in?'

'Door's open.'

'Can I talk to you for a minute?' Lisa asked.

Alessandra motioned the girl to the room's only chair and sat herself on the edge of the bed. She could tell at a glance that the teenager hadn't slept well.

'Shoot,' she said with an encouraging smile.

'I . . . I need to go into town with you today.'

'Well, you'd better hurry and get dressed, 'cause your dad wants to leave early——'

'Dad! I thought Jim would be driving you in . . . He always does.'

'Usually, but apparently Bart has an errand to run, so it makes sense that I go with him.'

Alessandra watched as the younger woman first twisted then untwisted her hands for several moments before she spoke again.

'Forget it. I can wait until next week.'

'Lisa, I realise you're angry with your father, but you can't keep on avoiding him.'

'It's not that. I don't want him to know where I'm going.' She cast a look of uncertainty towards the older woman. 'I want to go to the doctor's and he'll want to know why.'

'I see.' Alessandra thought she knew exactly why Lisa wanted to consult a doctor and why she didn't want her father to find out. 'Are you sure?'

'Sure? Of course I'm sure. Daddy will freak! You won't tell him, will you, Alessandra?'

Alessandra stood up and went to crouch by the girl's chair. Her heart went out to the kid. She could just imagine the fear the poor thing was feeling, but Lisa couldn't realistically expect her to end the conversation there.

'Lisa, you have to tell your father. This is something you have to discuss with him.'

'No way. It hasn't anything to do with him——'

'Oh, come on, Lisa! He's your father. You have to tell him. How far along are you?'

'What?'

'How advanced is the pregnancy?'

'*Pregnancy*! I'm not pregnant, Alessandra! That's what I'm trying to *avoid*!'

Alessandra sank to her knees and offered a silent thanks to the Lord. Raising her head, she smiled widely.

'Crossed wires in the worst way. Sorry, Lisa.'

'That's OK. But telling Dad I want to go on the Pill would be on a par to telling him I'm pregnant, believe me.'

'I don't think so. What method of contraception are you and Todd practising at the moment?'

'None . . .'

'Are you crazy, Lisa?' She wanted to shake the youngster; instead she ran anxious fingers through her short cropped hair. 'Talk about tempting fate!'

Lisa was shaking her head vigorously. 'We aren't sleeping together yet.'

Once again Alessandra congratulated herself on jumping the gun. She should have realised that Lisa was far too sensible to take such a risk.

'That's why I want to go on the Pill now. *Before* anything happens.'

'Smart girl. OK, listen, I still think it would be wise to discuss the matter with your father, but I can understand how you feel. At eighteen I felt the same way. What if I swap my next Saturday off with one of the guys and on Monday you and I can head into town for a shopping excursion and a visit to the doctor's?'

'You'd do that? You'd come with me?'

'Sure.'

Alessandra was hugged enthusiastically even before she'd finished speaking.

'Oh, Alessandra! You are terrific! Totally and absolutely terrific!'

'I'm glad one Cameron thinks so,' she said drily.

Bart was already in the Range Rover when Alessandra climbed into the front seat. Without looking at him, she tossed a casual 'Gidday' and reached for her seatbelt. Only when that was comfortably secure did she become aware that Bart was staring at her as if she had two heads.

'Bart?'

'My God, you're wearing a dress.'

'Skirt, actually.'

'Have you run out of jeans?'

She smiled at the first piece of teasing conversation she'd heard from him in a week, glad she hadn't chickened out and resorted to her daily uniform of Levis. He *had* noticed.

'I like a change every so often.'

He offered no further comment, gunning the engine to life, and they drove for six miles before the prickling silence became too much for Alessandra. She turned slightly in the seat, pulling her legs up under the calf-length skirt, to make herself more comfortable.

'I see your vow of silence is going well,' she said casually.

Bart, struggling not to laugh, cast her a quick glance.

'Oh, no...it's the shock of the skirt. I see,' Alessandra said with pseudo-sympathy.

He laughed.

'Sshh,' Alessandra said. 'Someone might hear you and get the idea that you don't find my presence quite so aggravating as you make out.'

'Is that what you think? That you aggravate me?'

'Sometimes.'

He arched an eyebrow below the brim of his stetson. 'Only sometimes?'

'Yeah. The rest of the time I *infuriate* you. True?'

Bart wondered how she would respond if he told her that while she did at times both aggravate and infuriate him, she turned him on *all* the time. He gripped the wheel as resentment of his attraction to her fought the need to tell her the truth: that he couldn't get her out of his head, that the scent of the magnolia oil she always wore was constantly with him, and that he was still kicking himself over the incident at the creek. Although he wasn't sure if it was because he'd started it or because he'd stopped it short of its natural conclusion.

'You puzzle me, Alessandra. I don't understand you.'

Alessandra laughed loudly.

'What's so funny?' he asked, not certain he wasn't the source of her amusement.

'Don't sound so concerned, Bart. If I had ten cents for every time someone has said that I'd be worth millions!'

'You have to admit you're not the conventional twenty-eight-year-old.'

'Conventional by whose standards?'

'Normal standards.'

'So not only am I aggravating, infuriating and unconventional, I'm also not normal...'

'I didn't mean any offence, Alessandra...'

'Ease up, Bart, I'm only stirring you,' she said, putting a conciliatory hand on his shoulder and hastily whipping it away as a shot of electricity rocketed up her arm.

'Stir... stirring me?' Bart struggled to get the words out and ignore the warmth her touch had ignited within him. Lord, she was *stirring* him all right!

'Teasing. Having a go at you. Egging you on.'

'Right,' Bart said and decided to change the subject. 'When we get to town I have to meet with Doug Shaffer about a bull he's interested in buying. Why don't you amuse yourself with some shopping for an hour and then I'll meet you at the bank?'

Alessandra knew that it made more sense than to have her carrying around the ranch's payroll while she killed time waiting for Bart, but the truth was she hated shopping. Oh, well, she could always hang out at the library and bone up on local history.

'Well, it's about time!'

Alessandra pounced on Bart as soon as he walked into the bank.

'One hour, you said. I've been standing here so flamin' long the security guard must think I'm casing the joint!'

'Sorry, I got held up.'

'Yeah, that's what the security guard thought was going to happen to him!'

Bart couldn't help the smile spreading across his face. She was so damn sexy when fury flashed through those peacock-blue eyes, and the unamused line of her mouth was a temptation all by itself. If he weren't so well known in the town he'd have hauled her off and kissed her senseless. In fact he was tempted to regardless.

'Listen, mate, would you like to wipe that stupid grin off your face and answer me?'

'What?' he replied.

She raised her eyes heavenward and sighed, but not loud enough to drown out the growl from her stomach.

'Pardon?' Bart said with a fake expression of shock.

'That's another thing,' she complained tersely. 'I've been here so long my stomach thinks my throat has been cut. Let's cash the salary cheque and go eat!' Grabbing Bart's wrist, she began leading him in the direction of the bank clerk.

Her touch sent rivers of fire rushing through his bloodstream and it took all of his will-power not to heave her into his arms and make love to her on the spot.

It wasn't until she was standing in front of the bank clerk that Alessandra became aware of her hold on Bart's wrist. She dropped it immediately.

'Sorry,' she apologised, wishing he would stop staring at her.

'Why are you sorry?'

He was standing only inches from her. There was no physical contact between them and yet she was incapable of either moving or looking away. Something was tightening in her throat and she couldn't speak beyond a husky whisper.

'For... dragging you about.'

'May I help you?' the bank clerk asked.

'Did I complain?'

'Excuse me, miss... May I help you?'

'No.'

'Then please move away. You're holding up the line.'

'Then don't apologise.'

'Fine.'

'Doug invited me to have lunch with him.'

'Oh.'

'Miss, would you please make a transaction or leave the line?'

'I told him I had to meet you, so he said to bring you along and he'd bring his wife. Do you mind?'

'If he brings his wife? Why should I?'

'Miss! You are holding up the line! People are waiting.'

'I mean do you mind if we have lunch with them?'

'No. But I'm not really dressed for a posh restaurant.'

'I think you look terrific.'

'Excuse me, sir, but could you please let the lady make her transaction?'

'Really?'

'Always.'

As Bart's head began to lower Alessandra raised herself on tip-toe and closed her eyes. Suddenly a heavy

object dropped on to her shoulder. Turning, she found
the bank security guard at her side.

'Madam, you have been in this bank for nearly two
hours already, but I doubt the people in the line behind
you have that much time to spare. Would you kindly
finish your business—your *banking business*, and move
on?'

'Sorry, Bill, my fault entirely. How are you doin'?'

Bart's pally greeting spared Alessandra from having
to answer the guard, but it didn't save her from the irritated glare of the bank clerk. Giving her most cheerfully friendly smile, she slid the cheque across the
counter.

Alessandra had eaten in some of the finest restaurants
of the world, with people of all social classes, but never
had she felt as uncomfortable as she did sitting opposite
Rachel Shaffer in this small but pleasant establishment
hundreds of miles from Brisbane. The woman was the
nastiest piece of goods Alessandra had ever had the mis-
fortune to meet. So far she'd managed to malign what
sounded like every female member of the local com-
munity, and to make matters worse she persisted in
calling her *Alexandra*. Glancing at Bart, she wondered
just how important the sale of this bull was to him, because for two cents she'd tell the bitch just exactly what
she thought of her. On second thoughts she'd do it for
nothing!

'Bart tells me you're quite a cowhand,' Doug Shaffer
said conversationally.

'Well, I must say it's nice to know one's boss appre-
ciates one's work. Perhaps I should ask for a rise?'

'Never hurts to try, I always say.' Doug gave her a
wink.

'Please, Doug, don't encourage her.' Bart smiled at
Alessandra. 'Otherwise I may have to increase the price
on Black George to compensate for the rise in her pay.'

'Ouch!' Doug said with a pained expression. 'On second thoughts, a rise might not be a good idea, my dear.'

'Really, Doug, I'm sure Alessandra is more than adequately *compensated* for her duties at Rough Rivers,' Rachel Shaffer chided her husband.

Alessandra quietly gripped the stem of her wine glass and forced a smile at the elegantly made-up redhead. Talk about mutton dressed up as lamb! The woman's mind was so far in the gutter that you'd need a fireman's ladder to get it out.

'I must say, Alessandra, that is a very—er—*interesting* skirt you have on. Terribly sixties. Of course, all the old stuff is back in...in some circles. Personally I always found it a rather *scruffy* era,' she said.

'I can barely remember the era,' Alessandra said sweetly. 'I was only a toddler, but my mother has told me about it.' She saw Bart quickly smother a chuckle.

'Actually I bought this skirt in Israel two years ago; from memory it cost me two pairs of cut-off jeans.'

'You've done a lot of travelling, Alessandra?' Doug enquired.

At least he was pleasant, she thought, giving him a genuine smile in appreciation.

'I got the bug at nineteen and haven't spent more than a couple of years, total, in Australia since.'

'You never went to college?' Rachel's question was weighted in horror.

'I studied at the University of Sydney for one year.' Alessandra shrugged. 'I opted for travel over study and freedom over money.'

'You have no desire to settle down and forgo the nomadic life you lead?' Rachel's tone was blatantly disapproving.

'At the moment I have no reason to settle down. Excuse me a moment, would you?'

Bart and Doug rose simultaneously, as Alessandra left the table.

Ooohh! That woman! She was a perfect example of what money and designer clothes couldn't do. Turning the cold tap on full strength, Alessandra held her wrists under the stream of water in an effort to cool her blood. She was just beginning to enjoy the solitude of the ladies' room when the overpowering smell of Yves Saint Laurent's Opium hit her nostrils. Anyone with real class knew one didn't wear Opium during the day!

'A bit tipsy, Alexandra?'

'No, Rachel, just a little overheated.'

The redhead lit a cigarette and drew back slowly, making a very obvious appraisal of the younger blonde. Alessandra watched the distaste her white off-the-shoulder blouse and vivid yellow embroidered skirt created in the woman's face. Her hand-woven sandals were dismissed in the same pithy manner.

'So you're Bart's latest?'

'Latest bookkeeper, I presume you mean.'

'Of course! Whatever did you think I meant?'

'I assumed, quite correctly, you meant lover.'

Rachel gave a nasty chuckle. 'You should be so lucky!'

For a fleeting second Alessandra wondered if this woman was speaking from experience. No, Bart had cows more appealing than Rachel Shaffer!

'I only hope that meeting you today isn't an indication my luck is taking a switch for the worse.' Alessandra reached for the door before adding sweetly, 'Oh, by the way, I love your hair. It must be *awfully* difficult to dye the roots black.'

Feeling better, she let the door swing shut on the woman's outraged gasp.

For most of the drive home the conversation had been spasmodic and hadn't touched on anything heavier than local history, Bart asking Alessandra about various things

that he'd read about in the library and oho telling him
of other events that had shaped this part of Australia.
But guilt was getting the better of her.

'How desperately do you want to sell Black George
to Doug?'

It was clear from his expression that her question
caught him by surprise.

'Well, it's not a case of being desperate. Just a matter
of good business. Why?'

'Because I think I might have cost you the sale.'

Bart sent her a puzzled look. 'If that was the case I'm
sure Doug wouldn't have invited us to the party they're
having Saturday night.'

Alessandra sat bolt upright and swore.

'Charming language——'

'Tell me you didn't accept! *Please* tell me you didn't
accept.'

Bart pulled to the side of the road and stopped the
engine.

'Of course I accepted. Why shouldn't I?'

'Tell me you didn't accept on my behalf.' Alessandra
saw his pained look. 'Bart, how could you? Oh, God!'

He ran an exasperated hand across his face.

'Alessandra, you were in the powder-room and Doug
said they were having a small party Saturday night and
would we come? I thought since you hadn't met many
of the folks from around these parts socially you might
like the opportunity.'

'Not if they're like Rachel Bitch-face Shaffer, I don't!'

'Ah, so that's it.'

She threw him a dirty look. 'Stop smirking.'

'Look, I know Rachel is a bit of a gossip and tends
to be a little snobby——'

'"A little snobby"? That's like saying that Jack
the Ripper was a little aggressive! Or that Hitler was a
little crazy!'

Alessandra's outrage was so comical that Bart let loose with uncontrolled laughter. It was, he decided, not improving the situation any, and with great effort he fought to control his mirth.

'You . . . you have to admit you gave as good . . . as you got! "I can barely remember the era, but my mother has told me about it." Hardly meek acceptance.' He was still chuckling.

'You think *that's* funny? Try this on for size . . . In the powder-room, she implied that I was your latest bedmate.' The laughter stopped. 'I thought that might kill your humour.'

'What did you say to that?'

'I told her I was your bookkeeper. Not that the truth is likely to stop her from spreading rumours.'

'Would it bother you that much?'

Something in his voice drew her eyes to his and suddenly she felt as if she were drowning in their cool pale blueness. Instinctively she knew he wasn't talking about how she'd feel as the subject of gossip.

'I wasn't the one who changed their mind down by the creek. Was I?'

'I want you, Alessandra. We both know that. What I don't understand is why I want you.'

'Gee, thanks,' she said.

'I'm trying to be honest with you, Alessandra,' Bart told her.

'Bull! You've tried to talk yourself out of having an affair with me by telling yourself you're not my type, but it hasn't worked. So now you're hoping that I'll make it easy for you by agreeing that we aren't suited and that it's best if we just ignore this . . . this sexual pull that we feel whenever we get within cooee of each other. Well, I agree. We *aren't* suited,' she said fervently.

'I take it you feel pretty strongly about all this.' Bart held her gaze as he ran a slow finger back and forth across her lips.

'Very,' she sighed. 'And if you don't hurry up and kiss me... I swear I'll go mad.'

Bart reached across to unbuckle her seatbelt, without taking his eyes from her face. Already his breathing was beginning to sound laboured and his shaky fingers were making hard work of a simple task.

Then Alessandra's hand moved to work with his and as if by magic the buckle released. He watched a tiny smile of triumph tug at the corners of her lipstick-free mouth.

'See,' she whispered, moving to him. 'We work well together.'

There was nothing tentative in the way Bart's mouth met hers and just for a second Alessandra wondered why she should have thought there would be. Then she was beyond any form of mental logic as his tongue slipped between her eagerly parted lips. A hint of coffee lingered in his mouth and its bitterness invited her excited tongue to slip deeper. Bart's responsive groan of pleasure sent waves of erotic warmth tumbling through her.

Bart was again stunned by the complete lack of shyness Alessandra displayed, but he was helpless to question it. Her hands were creeping ever so slowly up his back and he swore she was singeing the thin fabric of his shirt with every movement. Moving his head into the crook of her neck, he trailed his tongue along it and was rewarded not only by the softness he found there, but also by the strangely erotic magnolia scent that was essential to all his images of Alessandra.

'Oohh... yes, Bart, I love that.'

The breathless quality of her voice motivated him to explore the golden expanse of shoulder exposed by her blouse.

Alessandra let her head fall back as Bart's mouth continued its caress downward. At last he reached the elasticised top of her blouse and she waited without breathing for his tongue to renew its slick exploration. She waited, gnawed at by a need, such as she'd never known, for the feel of his mouth's sweet wetness against her. But it didn't come.

'Ba ... Bart?'

'Don't move,' he ordered softly, turning the ignition key with an unsteady hand. 'Unless I ... get this vehicle ... off the main ... road, we're gonna draw one hell of ... an audience.' His voice was a shaky as his hands.

Less than a minute later Bart brought the vehicle to a stop behind the ruins of what must have once been a storage shed of some description. Bart took her chin in his hands and kissed her gently.

Alessandra marvelled at how she had once thought him less than handsome. His face was without doubt the most beautiful she'd ever seen. There were fine lines at his eyes—character lines. Lines of strength, integrity and good humour.

'You haven't changed your mind, have you?'

She shook her head, smiling.

'Good. Now stay put for a minute,' Bart instructed, opening his door and striding towards the old building.

Despite the kinetic energy consuming her, Alessandra sat and watched as he made a quick check around the old building. He opened the rear of the 4 by 4 and spread an old blanket on the ground, before opening the passenger-side door and holding out his hand.

She took, it feeling like some fairy-tale princess. When she would have taken a step towards the blanket, Bart swept her up into his arms as easily as if she weighed nothing. No man had ever treated her so gallantly, and, as a one-time hard-core feminist, she was surprised to find herself loving every minute of it.

'How will you explain it if you throw your back out?' she teased, drawing an invisible line across the width of his shoulders and delighting in the ripple of muscle beneath her finger.

'I've carried heifers that weigh more than you.'

'Well, there's a backhanded compliment if ever I've heard one! Do you say that to all the girls?'

Gently he lowered her on to the blanket and positioned himself on his elbows above her.

'I don't make a habit of this, Alessandra.'

'No, I can tell. If you did you wouldn't have fought so hard to prevent it.'

His fingers played across the top of her blouse, barely skimming her skin and yet working the fabric slowly but surely lower.

'But you, you never fought it, did you, Alessandra?'

He asked the question just as he caught the elastic beneath her left breast, and her answer was lost in his awed gasp.

'I never fight the inevitable.'

He smiled. 'Somehow I can't see you as a model of docile acceptance.'

'I'm never docile, Bart.'

His mouth closed over the gem-hard peak of her breast and Alessandra's knees jerked up in reflex to the power of the sensation he created within her. Never had she experienced such a surge of raw sensuality as he eased her back, carefully removing her blouse, his touch inflaming her body with just the slightest contact. She could hardly breathe while for several moments he admired the firm, yet soft perfection that lay bare before only him, God and the Australian sun.

Her fingers moved quickly to the buttons of his shirt and deftly she undid them one by one, pausing only to reef the fabric free of his jeans and undo the remaining two. She ran her finger from the base of his throat down his sternum to the muscular firmness of his belly and revelled in the granite strength layered under smooth but heated masculine flesh and a thatch of thick, silky hair.

In a fluid motion Bart shrugged clear of the shirt, but Alessandra had no time to gaze idly at what she knew was a magnificent chest, for he claimed her mouth with a passion she'd known only in her most recent dreams.

His hands roamed and caressed her breasts with such gentleness that she marvelled that they were the same hands which bore the evidence of his hard labour on the ranch. When he moved them beneath the elastic band of her skirt and across the smooth softness of her lower abdomen she was helpless to control the excited shudders of anticipation that coursed through her. She felt Bart roll off her and in a distant part of her mind registered the snap of his jeans opening.

Her eyes absorbed every detail of his previously hidden lower body as he knelt and edged his jeans down. The thatch of hair narrowed like an arrow head towards the conspicuous bulge in his briefs, and her unspoken phallic analogy only served to moisten the passage of her femininity more. Her body demanded that she touch him, and she obeyed it, rising to her knees in front of him.

Bart froze in fascination as she lightly kissed him then huskily told him not to move. Then slowly, oh, ever so slowly, she kissed every inch of skin from his knees to shoulders. The sensations she was concocting within him were, he was sure, more potent than any mind-bending drug known to science.

No longer could he stand such delicious torture without the threat of prematurely denying her. Taking her in his arms, he eased them both back to the ground.

'Lord, Alessandra, you're part witch, I swear... I've never had to fight so hard for control...'

'Don't fight...go with it...'

'I will as soon as I get this damned thing on...'

Opening her eyes, it took her a moment to focus on what Bart's fingers were struggling with, before she recognised the small foil packet for what it was...a condom. She put her hand out towards him, palm upwards, but saw the hesitation in his eyes.

'Let me.'

He was too bemused to say anything as he watched her tear open the gold foil, then carefully remove and inspect the item to make sure she had it the right way.

'Mind you, I am on the Pill and I just happen to have my blood-donor card in my wallet if you want to check it out...' She paused to look at his face.

He shook his head. 'Put it on.'

Alessandra tried not to show how hurt she was by his insistence. Of course it was only sensible as far as he was concerned—he barely knew her—but then again she only had his word that he didn't sleep around; still, as surely as they lay here beneath a scorching Australian sun and bright blue sky, if Bart had said it was raining, she'd have believed him.

Her hand was shaking and she motioned for Bart to remove his briefs. When he did so the readiness of him caused her to gasp audibly.

Bart was sure he would burst with pride at the admiration he heard in the quick intake of her breath, but as she began to roll the condom on to him with gentle fingers and slow tenderness his pride wasn't the only thing he was worried about exploding.

'For pity's sake! Alessandra, hurry up...or you'll...have simply...wasted your time.'

'Done.' She gave him a shy smile. It was the first time she'd performed such an action, but doing it for Bart had seemed the most natural thing in the world. He pulled her urgently against him and seized her mouth with a heat that turned her loins to a molten pool of desire. Apart from her lace panties, she was totally naked, and it didn't take Bart more than a second to discard those. He rolled her on to her back and then proceeded to trail kisses the entire length of her body. Her back arched without any conscious instruction from her brain as logical thought lagged behind her physical need for fulfilment. Her blood seemed to roar as his mouth worked its silken magic back up to her throat and his fingers trailed the inside of her thighs and beyond with insidious slowness.

'Bart...please. Now...now! I can't wait!'

'Just a second, honey...'

She was dimly aware of Bart moving over her, but his entry into her was almost simultaneous.

'Aahh...'

'Easy, take it easy...' Bart wasn't sure which of them he was endeavouring to slow down, because he had never experienced such a furiously aroused passion. For this first time in his life he was a slave to his most basic instincts. He was stunned by the need she created in him, the need to have more and more of the taste, feel and scent of her, and the sensual thrill of hearing her whispered, 'Yes...oh, Bart...yes, yes...yes.'

Alessandra was sure that this was as close to heaven as she was ever going to get, yet surely anything this wonderful, this potent, was beyond the powers of an earthly male? Tiny explosives were sparking deep in the centre of her sensuality and gradually growing in intensity...merging as one and moving...moving not just through her body but into her head... She struggled for a second, not quite comfortable with or certain of this foreign, magical feeling, but Bart's voice reached her...

'Go with it, honey...enjoy it and just ride it out...easy, easy, honey...'

Bart...darling, wonderful Bart...could he feel this too...? Could he see...the stars and...and rainbows that were so close...so close that if she just rea...ched out she could...?

He held her tightly as the final shudder of climactic fulfilment quaked from her body and only then did he empty himself into her wet warmth, with a rush that refuted his patience until then.

No woman had ever evoked such desperate urgency from his lovemaking. Alessandra MacKellar was something else. He gently brushed the damp tendrils of hair from her forehead and was rewarded with the most incredibly beautiful smile he had ever seen...

CHAPTER FIVE

FOR the first time in her life Alessandra understood how one could be struck speechless, the sheer power of the experience having robbed her of control over her brain and vocal cords. The touch of his hand against her damp forehead drew her eyes back to his and in them she saw the aftermath of his passion. Was he too surprised by the intensity of what had happened between them? Certainly the quiet, easygoing impression he usually displayed conveyed none of the unrestrained enthusiasm or experience he'd shown in his lovemaking. Alessandra was confused for more reasons than simply the fact he'd evoked such an unfettered response from her. Now he seemed uncomfortable with her.

He pulled away and sat up, linking his arms around his knees, his eyes focused on the horizon.

'Why did you offer to put the condom on?' he asked.

'I wanted to...to touch you,' she said honestly, feeling herself blush.

'Did it bother you?'

'Of course not! Did it bother you?'

'Nope. More like surprised.'

'Why?'

He shrugged. 'I guess it's not something I'd expect of a lady.'

At his words, Alessandra knew she'd just made one of the biggest mistakes of her life. Bart was silent for some seconds, before reaching for his clothes.

'Come on, we'd better get back.'

The drive home was made in total silence.

* * *

When Lisa told her Bart probably wouldn't be in for dinner Alessandra's heart plummeted to her knees. She hadn't seen him since he'd dropped her off at the house; this unexplained absence and his reserve on the trip home, after their unabashed passion, was filling her with doubts she didn't want to have. Looking down at the plate of cold beef and salad lying before her, she felt her stomach turn. She closed her eyes, willing the nervous nausea away.

Oh, God, please don't let Bart regret what happened today. I couldn't stand it if he were to act as if nothing happened, or...

'Sorry I'm late. We're having a problem with one of the mares.'

Alessandra's head jerked around to where Bart stood, her eyes absorbing his presence as greedily as the desert absorbed water. At first her gaze was returned with one she didn't recognise, then his face broke into a shy smile and warmed her to her toes. Instantly she decided she wanted to spend the rest of her life waiting for this man to come in for dinner each night.

'Alessandra, do you feel OK? You've been looking awfully strange since we sat down?'

Lisa's words broke the spell between them.

'Have I? Funny, I've never felt better. In fact——' she darted a cheeky look at Bart '—I feel positively——'

'You're imagining things, Lisa,' Bart deliberately cut in. 'Alessandra looks fine to me.'

Lisa shrugged and returned her attention to her meal. Bart hovered halfway between the door and the table, knowing the smart thing to do was simply to sit down and begin his meal, but more hungry for the taste of the beautiful blue-eyed blonde seated at the table. Yet with his daughter present he really didn't have a choice. He pulled back his chair and sat down.

'Have you finished doing the wages?'

'Yeah.' Alessandra gave him an impish grin. 'It took me ages, though. For some reason I couldn't concentrate on what I was doing.'

Bart tried to smother a smile as Lisa looked in his direction.

'Speaking of "ages", you pair spent a long time in town today. What kept you?'

'Umm . . .'

'Your dad's meeting ran overtime and in the end we had lunch with the Shaffers.' Alessandra rushed to Bart's rescue when it looked as if Lisa's question might cause him to choke.

'I mean after that. Doug Shaffer rang here expecting you'd be home.' Lisa was oblivious to the look that passed between Alessandra and Bart. 'If I'd known you were going to do more than just cash the wages and meet with Doug Shaffer I'd have come along and gone to a movie.'

'What did Doug want?' Bart asked, in what Alessandra knew to be a desperate attempt to change the subject.

'Just said to be sure to tell you that the party starts at eight and that he's looking forward to showing Alessandra some real Aussie hospitality.'

'What's he going to do—lock Rachel in her room?' Alessandra muttered.

'Pardon?' Lisa asked, looking lost.

'Alessandra and Rachel didn't exactly hit it off,' Bart explained wryly.

'The only thing I'd like to hit off that woman would be her malicious smirk. As for her unfounded accusations . . .' Alessandra stopped guiltily. Rachel's accusations were no longer unfounded. She looked at Bart.

'What accusations?' Lisa probed.

'She said——'

'You know Rachel, Lisa. Gossip is her middle name,' Bart said, smoothly interrupting Alessandra.

Lisa laughed and pushed herself from the table. 'Middle name? Dad, gossip is Rachel Shaffer's career!'

Bart returned to the stables immediately after dinner and Lisa challenged Alessandra to a game of Trivial Pursuit, but Alessandra's brain was light-years away from the game. After she'd answered the question, 'Who's smarter than the average bear?' with, 'Koala,' and credited Lyndon Johnston with being the first president of the United States, Lisa suggested they abandon the game and go to bed.

'Dad'll probably be all night down at the stable,' she advised from the foot of the stairs.

Hardly the news Alessandra wanted to hear. She needed to talk to Bart. Needed to find out if his hopes for their relationship were the same as hers. Her hopes. Lord, but she'd never felt so insecure or unsure of herself. In the past when her mother had asked, 'But don't you want to settle down? Don't you want to marry and have children? Provide yourself with some security for the future?' Alessandra had always dismissed the questions with a shrug of her shoulders and, 'If it happens, it happens, but I'm happy with my life just the way it is now.'

She hadn't been lying. It was nearly ten years since she'd fled Sydney, in an effort to put Jenni's death, family demands and her beliefs into perspective. It had taken almost twelve months to come to terms with all that had happened in her turbulent eighteenth year, but finally she knew that if she had to please anyone it was herself. New countries, new friends and new experiences were what excited Alessandra and she'd spent the last nine years pursuing them with unflagging enthusiasm. If at times she felt the need for family, she made a pit stop in Sydney, reacquainted herself with her brothers and parents, and met any new sisters-in-law or nieces and nephews that had cropped up in her absence. Whatever money she managed to save while living at home became her means to securing another airline ticket to adventure. What she'd learned from hands-on experience with other cultures was far more valuable than any university degree. The only security she needed was knowing that what she was doing was what was right for Alessandra Elizabeth MacKellar.

That was until today. Until a man named Bart Cameron had shown her she needed something more than just her freedom and absolute belief in herself.

'Why aren't you in bed?'

He stood propped against the door-frame, looking magnificent in filthy blue jeans, a shirt stained from sweat and grime, and with his hair sticking out in all directions.

'I was waiting for you.'

Bart moved to where she sat on the sofa and gently held her chin. She was beautiful. For weeks he had been haunted by those wide blue eyes and their long blue lashes twenty-four hours a day and now he would be haunted by the memory of her naked flesh against his own and the magnolia scent of her.

'I need a shower.'

'I need you.'

Her lips tasted of passion and desire and he gave himself willingly to the kiss. Her tongue darted randomly about his mouth and teased his with its sweetness. The tiny groan she gave, as he eased her down on to the softness of the sofa, ignited his blood. Beneath his fingers he felt the soft skin of her belly grow hot as he stroked a lazy pattern back and forth, but the languid rhythm of his hand quickened as he felt the moistness of her tongue sear a path to his neck. Erotic sensations crept their way through his body and weakened his capacity to breathe evenly or control his desire. Tiny murmurs of delight welcomed his touch beneath the waistband of her skirt, further stoking his passion.

Alessandra felt her muscles contract with excitement as Bart's fingers moved sensuously closer to the laced top of her bikini pants. Linking her hands behind his neck, she arched her body as his hand cupped the area between her thighs and her slick dampness told them both of her hunger. His slow, stroking tenderness spiralled through every cell of her body and she could do nothing to decelerate her wanton, desperate need to absorb more of him.

He moved off her so quickly that Alessandra momentarily thought someone must have entered the room, but they were alone.

'Bart?'

'I'm sorry, Alessandra.'

'Sorry?'

Bart's grim expression told her the moment was gone. Swinging her feet to the ground, she straightened her clothes and waited for some explanation for his emotional turn-around. Her heart shivered as she watched an expression of distaste move across his face, rapidly followed by one of suppressed anger. Was she the cause?

'Don't look like that,' he told her.

'Like what?'

'Like you don't know what the problem is here.'

'I wasn't aware there *was* a problem.'

Bart sent her an aggrieved look, running his hand through his hair.

'We both know what happened this afternoon was inevitable, and I'd be lying if I said I wasn't attracted to you.'

'But...' Alessandra prompted, even though the knotting in her stomach told her she didn't want to hear any more.

'But I'm not a hypocrite. I can't preach to Lisa about the shallowness of purely physical relationships while I'm involved in one right under her nose.'

Alessandra gripped her stomach as a wave of nausea washed over her. Strong as the desire was to run from the room, her legs were too weak to comply. She tried to use controlled breathing to block out his voice, but it penetrated with knife-like precision.

'Unlike you, I'm not used to casual affairs. I know I agreed to you staying on until Mrs Wilcox returns, but in the circumstances it might be better if you left. Naturally, I'll be happy to give you a reference, and with your capabilities you shouldn't have trouble getting another job.'

Anger was rising so quickly inside her that Alessandra feared she would explode. Shallow... Purely physical... Casual... Affairs. The key words hammered away at her brain. He'd barely side-stepped whore and trollop, she thought. On top of that he fully expected her to just ride off into the sunset, armed with a recommendation from him that she was good at her job! Then again, he might not even bother to mention her accounting skills, just the fact that she was an easy lay! Oooohhh! She wanted to kill the sanctimonious pig! She wanted to mince him into little pieces and feed him to his livestock! Instead she got to her feet and forced herself to laugh. It sounded almost genuine.

'Whoa! Listen, mate, you promised me a job for three months. Now if you want to fire me say so, but don't expect me to quit a perfectly good, well paying job simply because *you're emotionally stunted*! If what happened between us was so bloody *shallow*, then I can't see why you're making such a bloody issue out of it! I——'

'Alessan——'

'I'm more than capable of controlling my libido, *Mr Cameron*, but if you can't then you'll have to fire me. Because I . . . won't . . . quit!'

'Alessandra, are you listening to me?'

Lisa's voice brought the doctor's waiting-room back into focus.

'What? Oh, sorry, I didn't realise you were through with the doctor. Did everything go OK?' Alessandra asked, knowing the teenager had been nervous.

'I guess so. I've got a prescription.'

'Let's go, then. Do you have any more shopping you want to do?'

'Only at the chemist's,' Lisa said shyly.

'OK, we'll do that, then grab a cup of coffee before we head back to the ranch.'

The thick *cappuccino* reminded Alessandra of the coffee-shop she and her mother often frequented when she was in Sydney. Several times during the last couple of days she'd found herself thinking of Sydney and realised it was because she needed to remind herself that, despite all her travelling, she really did have a home, that Rough Rivers and Bart Cameron would soon fade to nothing more than travel memories. She hoped so at any rate.

'It's too bad you had to miss the Shaffers' party the other night. I heard it was quite a bash,' Lisa commented.

'Really? Did your dad say that?'

'He might have, but who'd know, the way he's been grunting and growling every time he opens his mouth these days. Do men go through change of life, Alessandra?'

Alessandra coughed violently as a mouthful of coffee wedged in her throat; by the time she'd regained her composure her eyes were watering.

'Are you OK?' Lisa enquired, patting her gently on the back.

'Lisa, warn me when you are going to ask totally unexpected questions like that.'

'Sorry.'

'Your father is thirty-eight. I'm not sure whether there is a male equivalent to menopause, but even so I'd say Bart was a little young for it.'

'Well, he's sure acting weird. Saturday night he caught Todd and me kissing on the porch and didn't say a word. Not even when I went inside.'

'Glass-house syndrome,' Alessandra muttered.

'What?'

'Nothing, Lisa. He's probably realised that you're old enough to make your own decisions and smart enough to make the right ones. I really do think you should tell him you're using contraception.'

'No way! The fact that I'm taking the Pill will automatically translate that I'm sleeping with Todd in Dad's mind,' Lisa said fervently.

'Well, it's up to you, but I think you're wrong.'

Lisa's face said she doubted this. Although tempted to pursue the issue, Alessandra decided that it was wiser to wait a while. There were other things of which Lisa should be made aware.

'Did the doctor explain everything about what taking the Pill implies, about what it does and what it *doesn't* do?'

'She told me that I'm not protected for the first month, so alternative precautions should be taken. And that I must be sure to read the instructions carefully and follow them to the letter,' Lisa said.

'Good. You do realise that these days you have to worry about more than just pregnancy if you're sexually active, don't you?' Alessandra asked and waited for Lisa's nod before continuing. 'There are also a couple of curve balls that nature can throw you that will negate the Pill.'

'Such as?'

'We'll talk about it on the way home. Finish your coffee and let's hit the frog and toad.'

'Frog and toad?'

'Sometimes I think you Yanks have no imagination! Let's hit the *road*. Rhyming slang. I'll teach you some on the way so you can dazzle your friends and confuse your father!'

Lisa laughed. 'I don't think I could be as good as you are at it.'

'Bull. Rhyming slang is easy.'

'No, I meant at *confusing Dad*!'

The rain continued to bucket down and Alessandra leaned even lower over Pewter's neck. Jim had said that if the weather turned sour to make for the derelict shack and sit out the worst of it there.

Unfortunately, Alessandra suspected that by the time she reached it 'the worst of it' would be over. She was drenched, although as much from perspiration as from the driving rain, for even though the all-weather coat protected her from neck to ankle against the rain the January heat didn't make for comfort. Neither did the dozens of cuts she had on her hands.

Since lunch she and Dunc, one of the younger hands, had been mending the extreme northern fences and they'd all but finished when Dunc had slashed his hand on the rusty wire. If she'd been smart, Alessandra observed in retrospect, she'd have headed back with Dunc and probably missed the storm. She would have if she didn't feel as if Bart Cameron was just waiting for her to slack off on her work so he could justify firing her. Even so, she'd been stupid to try and finish the fencing alone when Jim had predicted a storm. His forecasting was nearly always spot on the money. She just hoped to God his directions would turn out the same way! How much further could the damn shack be?

As if her thoughts had conjured it up, the dim watery outline of a cabin appeared on her left.

'I reckon an ark might be more appropriate, eh, Pewter?' she commented to the bedraggled horse as she tied his reins to an upright supporting a weathered porch, before entering the dilapidated main building.

The Waldorf it ain't! she thought, casting her eyes around the single room that was the entire cabin. A battered bunk with what the world's greatest optimist might have called a mattress, a lop-sided table and three battered chairs were the room's focal points, since all they had to compete with were a fireplace, blackened by what seemed like a century of soot, and a small doorless cupboard housing a couple of aged cups and a billy can. A layer of dust coated everything, then, because it had nowhere else to settle, it hung in the air. Alessandra told herself not to be ungrateful—at least it was a shelter of sorts. Turning, she went out and unsaddled her horse, then quietly surveyed the sky in all directions. The rain showed no sign of easing. Swearing under her breath, she carried her saddle back inside.

Two hours later there was still no break in the thick grey sky and Alessandra figured she had two choices. The first was to stay put until morning, an idea that had her hungry stomach growling in protest, the second being to start for home before it got too dark and hope she wasn't drowned on the way.

After riding for ten minutes she pondered the wisdom of opting for drowning over starvation, when discomfort and fatigue were fast overpowering her need for food. Again she cursed her stubborn pride that had made finishing the fence such a goddamn important issue. Bart Cameron would get just as much mileage out of her arriving back with pneumonia as he would have if she'd left the fence half done. Even more! She could just see his face... *She could just see his face!*

Oh, great! Why was it the ground never opened up when you wanted it to? She reined to a halt and waited silently as he pulled alongside her.

'Didn't Jim tell you to wait in the old squatters' shack?'

'I didn't think he meant indefinitely,' Alessandra replied, annoyed by the enormous sense of relief she felt at his unexpected appearance. For several moments they sat astride their mounts in consistent drizzling rain, assessing one another, before a clap of thunder spurred Bart to life.

'Come on,' he muttered tersely, moving his horse past hers. 'Let's get back to the cabin; sitting in the rain only makes your earlier actions seem less stupid.'

'Nobody asked you to come up here,' she retorted to his back as Pewter followed him.

'Ha! That's what you think!' he called over his shoulder. 'Jim was ready to send out a rescue team bigger than anything they saw in the San Francisco earthquake, and both Marilyn and Lisa would have lynched me if I'd left you out here alone.'

'Marilyn?' Alessandra motioned Pewter into a quicker stride and drew alongside Bart.

'Yeah. My big sister's dropped in for a surprise visit all the way from California!'

'Ripper!' she exclaimed. 'I really enjoyed the time I spent with her in LA. She's a great lady, your sister.'

Bart looked down into the radiant face half shadowed by a battered hat with water dripping from its wide brim. Her smile was such a contrast to her bedraggled appearance that he couldn't suppress one of his own.

'I seem to be surrounded by them lately.'

Alessandra felt her heart lurch. His words implied that he thought her a great lady too, but all too quickly his mouth thinned as if he was regretting his remark.

Alessandra again felt cold, and not because she was wet.

Bart was all business when they reached the shack and it was only quick reflexes which allowed Alessandra to catch the large plastic carrier-bag Bart tossed to her.

'Dry clothes for you. Lisa packed them.'

'Thanks.'

'There's some coffee in the Thermos, compliments of Marilyn. Pour some while I see if I can get this fire started.'

Usually Bart's tersely issued commands would have drawn Alessandra's sarcasm, but she was too grateful for his presence and the promise of something hot to drink.

'I couldn't find any matches earlier, so you can forget the fire idea.'

The words were no sooner out of her mouth than she heard the sound of a match being struck.

'Were you a Boy Scout or something?' she teased, handing him a steaming cup of coffee as he sat on his heels encouraging the small flame in the fireplace to bigger things.

'It's common sense to carry matches out here,' he said, taking the cup of coffee she held to him. 'Thanks. My God, your hands!'

She looked down at the mass of scratches and dried blood covering both sides of her hands. They looked ugly, but at least the stinging had stopped...well, almost.

'Dammit, Alessandra, why weren't you wearing gloves?' he demanded when she pulled away from him.

She wondered, if she'd been wearing a pair now, whether they'd have lessened the wattage of the electrical charge his touch had sent through her body.

'I lost them the other day. I was going to buy new ones when I went into town this week. It's no big deal, just a few scratches. Besides, Dunc had gloves on and he fared a lot worse than me.'

'You should have borrowed a pair. God knows there are plenty on the ranch.'

'I prefer to work without gloves than wear a pair ten times too big. If you don't watch that fire you're going to lose it,' she warned, successfully moving the conversation from herself.

Standing behind him allowed her the luxury of watching the way his muscular frame tested the soft chambray of his shirt. His physique was magnificent and she wanted to ease her hands over every square centimetre of it. It wasn't fair that she should feel so strongly attracted to a man who held such a low opinion of her.

She'd never considered herself to be God's gift to men and disapproval had never bothered her before. If someone didn't like her as they found her it was their problem, not hers. But suddenly Bart Cameron's approval was what she sought most in the world—after Bart Cameron himself!

'Dry yourself off and get changed; I'll wait on the porch.'

His words startled her out of her reverie.

'What about you?'

'I'm fine. When you're through I'll dry out in front of the fire. If we're lucky, by the time we've finished eating the weather should have cleared enough for us to make tracks for home.'

'And if we aren't lucky?' she questioned with a sly glance towards the one and only bunk in the cabin.

'I've got a sleeping-bag and a blanket.'

'Oh.'

'Alessandra, don't look for trouble. Just hurry up and dry off,' he ordered, slamming the door behind him.

CHAPTER SIX

BART sat with his right foot resting on his thigh, switching his focus from his coffee-cup to the fire and back again. Apart from offering to bathe her hands, he'd not spoken a word since he'd come back inside fifteen minutes earlier. Alessandra had had enough.

'Is the silent treatment your way of punishing me because you had to come rescue me, or what?'

He moved his eyes to her face and couldn't quite manage to suppress a grin.

'Actually I was curious to see how long *you* could go without exercising your vocal cords.' He made a production of checking his watch. 'Thirteen minutes, twenty seconds. Is that a record?'

'Very funny! I'll have you know I can go for hours without talking... when I'm asleep.'

'Are you sure about that?' Bart asked.

'Very.'

Bart saw the momentary far-away look in her eyes and wondered about the smile her thoughts had obviously prompted. Its soft warmth made him want to know its cause.

'What's so amusing?' he asked, but she laughed and shook her head, dismissing the importance of her reflections. 'Tell me...'

'My older brothers used to talk in their sleep regularly. You wouldn't believe some of the things they would say! When I was about twelve years old I used to slip into their rooms with a tape recorder in the hope of securing a juicy bit of info with which to blackmail them.'

'Nice kid.'

GET 4 BOOKS
A FLUFFY DUCK
AND A MYSTERY GIFT

Return this card, and we'll send you 4 specially selected Mills & Boon romances absolutely FREE! We'll even pay the postage and packing for you!

We're making this offer to introduce you to the benefits of Reader Service: FREE home delivery of brand-new romances at least a month before they're available in the shops, FREE gifts and a monthly Newsletter packed with information.

Accepting these FREE books places you under no obligation to buy, you may cancel at any time simply by writing to us — even after receiving just your free shipment.

← TEAR OFF AND POST THIS CARD TODAY ←

Yes, please send me 4 free Mills & Boon romances, a fluffy duck and a mystery gift. I understand that unless you hear from me, I will receive 6 superb new titles every month for just £1.99* each postage and packing free. I am under no obligation to purchase any books and I may cancel or suspend my subscription at any time, but the free books and gifts will be mine to keep in any case.

(I am over 18 years of age).

4A5R

Ms/Mrs/Miss/Mr _____

Address _____

_____

_____ Postcode _____

Get 4 books a fluffy duck and mystery gift FREE!

SEE OVER FOR DETAILS

POST THIS CARD TODAY

Harlequin Mills & Boon
FREEPOST
P. O. Box 70
Croydon
Surrey
CR9 9EL

No stamp needed

Offer closes 31st October 1995. We reserve the right to refuse an application. *Prices and terms subject to change without notice. Offer valid in U.K. and Eire only and is not available to current subscribers of this series. Overseas readers please write for details. Southern Africa write to: IBS Private Bag X3010, Randburg 2125.

You may be mailed with offers from other reputable companies as a result of this application. If you would prefer not to share in this opportunity, please tick box. ☐

'Hey,' she said innocently, 'what are sisters for?'

'Did you ever get anything... juicy?'

She laughed then nodded and Bart found himself unable to look away from the bright blue of her delighted eyes.

'What?'

'Now, Bart, what kind of self-respecting blackmailer would reveal a secret she'd been well reimbursed for keeping, um?'

He raised a sceptical eyebrow. 'The kind who would offer the information to a higher bidder.' She looked momentarily stunned and just a tad guilty. He pounced on her reaction.

'Ah! So you did play both ends against the middle!'

'Well, maybe once or twice,' she admitted sheepishly. 'But I was just a kid.'

'What if they'd tried the same thing on you?'

Alessandra gave a triumphant smirk, 'No way. I never talk in my sleep. My folks always used to tease the boys about it, but never me. Can you believe that all five of them used to indulge in dreamtime ravings? Perhaps it's a hereditary trait with men in my family,' she suggested thoughtfully.

'Living with you, it's more likely they never got a chance to get a word in while they were awake.'

She poked out her tongue. 'That was *their* standard excuse.'

'Well, I'd certainly buy it!' Bart teased. 'Tell me about your family. Do you get on with them?'

His question surprised her.

'Of course I do. Why would you ask that?'

'It's just I can't imagine why anyone would choose to leave their family and travel the world alone.' Bart saw a flicker of pain flash across her pretty pixie-like face, and it caused such a raw ache in his guts that he decided he didn't ever want to see it again. 'Look, let's change the subject.'

'No. Really, the subject isn't taboo. I adore my family and I'm conceited enough to believe they love me too. It's just that I didn't turn out quite the way they expected.'

'Ah. They weren't expecting a rebel,' Bart commented, causing her to laugh.

'I was always a bit wild, and growing up with five older brothers made me both spoilt and a tomboy. As for being a rebel, well, every one of the MacKellar kids fell into that category at some stage. Ask my mum; you wouldn't believe some of the stunts my brothers used to pull!' She shrugged as if unable to find the words to continue, but then did so. 'I guess the only difference between my brothers and me is that they went on to lead basically conformist-type lives, while I became what my father calls a terminal gypsy.'

'Why?' He saw that his question, although the natural one, seemed to leave Alessandra floundering for an answer.

'Why not?' she countered, giving a shrug and a smile that seemed to lack her usual commitment to trying to stop his heart. He felt she was deliberately avoiding stating her reasons, but before he could pursue them she had moved the conversation onward.

'Despite the fact I travel so much, we're a very close family.' She smiled. 'And though I'd never admit it to them, at times I miss my brothers' well intentioned advice.'

'Why do I have this feeling most of what they say would be ignored anyway?' he teased.

'I can't imagine,' Alessandra responded with theatrical innocence.

'Which brother is married to Marilyn's friend?'

'Greg. He and Lacey are utterly devoted to each other. Greg's an ex-pro Rugby League player, which is football——' Alessandra began to explain.

'I know. It's a great game!'

'Really? Even Yanks who've heard of the game aren't usually interested. How come you are?'

'When my uncle was serving in Korea, his platoon challenged an Australian one to a game of American football and beat them. So the Aussies wanted a rematch, but it had to be Rugby League. My uncle told me all about it,' Bart explained. 'About a million times!' he added fondly.

'So?'

'So what?'

'So who won?' she demanded.

'Would you believe me if I said we did?'

'Not in a million years.'

'Uncle Phil reckoned it was the toughest game of football he'd ever come across and that the Aussies whipped their tails.'

'Naturally,' Alessandra said haughtily, then smiled.

It wasn't a false smile or a planned smile, it was a smile that always seemed to bubble out when he was least expecting it. As usual Bart had to fight the urge to pull her into his arms and make love to her until he died from exhaustion. Instead he encouraged her to continue talking. As usual Alessandra didn't need much encouragement. It didn't take her long to finish telling him about the rest of her brothers, and before he knew it she was asking him questions he didn't want to answer. Although why he couldn't say.

'Tell me about Lisa's mother. What was she like?'

Bart stood and moved to the fire, as if he felt he needed to distance himself from her presence. The action hurt Alessandra more than she wanted to admit. Evidently, he still felt enormous pain remembering his wife. He had obviously loved her a great deal, and Alessandra was disgusted with herself for feeling the stirrings of jealousy towards the deceased woman. His voice was tight and subdued when finally he spoke.

'Kathleen was even more beautiful than Lisa. She had that clear white skin that was almost translucent and the most enormous almond-shaped eyes. Her eyes had a brightness that meant if you didn't know her you'd have sworn she was high on drugs. They'd light up the moment she woke and stay that way until she went to sleep. Even when she was sad or ill her eyes never seemed to loose their vividness.' Bart's lips eased into a gentle smile. 'Kath was fifteen when I first met her, at a cousin's wedding. She was wearing a floor-length dress of the softest fabric I'd ever seen . . . I can't remember what she called it, but there were layers and layers of the stuff in the palest pink I'd ever seen . . .' He paused, aware that Alessandra had muttered something. 'What?'

'Chiffon. It sounds like chiffon.'

He shrugged. 'I can't remember. But I do know that up until then I'd never imagined a girl could be so beautiful. Or so, so elegant and feminine. I was walking twenty feet tall when it became apparent that she thought I was OK too.'

As curious as she'd been about Lisa's mother before, Alessandra wished to heaven Bart would shut up now! The last thing she wanted was to hear him speaking in a voice laced with undeniable love for another woman. It was tearing her apart. She tried to mentally block out his words, yet they continued to permeate her mind.

'Try as they might, Kath's parents couldn't keep us apart. I was her mother's worst nightmare as far as potential son-in-laws went, but she knew she didn't have a snowball's chance in hell of stopping me from marrying Kathleen.'

He moved away from the fireplace to roam the room, not once looking at her, and Alessandra felt as if she'd become invisible as he lost himself in long ago memories. He spoke aloud, but it seemed to be more for his benefit than hers. Alessandra had never felt more alone in her entire life.

'My uncle died, leaving me the ranch, only weeks before we were to marry, so I couldn't spare the time for a honeymoon. Kath's parents had paid for us to go to Hawaii for two weeks, but it was impossible.'

He paused and she almost cried at the look of regret that washed across his weathered features. She'd never seen him look so desolate.

'Kathleen had always dreamed of going to Hawaii and that was the only reason I swallowed my pride and agreed to accepting such an extravagant gift in the first place. But when my uncle died I felt I had too much on my plate here to waste time sunning in Hawaii. I promised I'd take her the following year no matter what.' Bart ran a weary hand across his face, then looked at her. 'You've been to Hawaii. What's it like?'

'You . . . never ended up going?'

He shook his head. 'Kathleen died before I had a chance to make good my promise.'

'Oh, God.' Her words were a strangled gasp. 'I'm sorry.'

'Yeah. Me too.'

For several seconds a heavy silence filled the room as neither spoke nor moved. Suddenly Alessandra felt as if she would pass out from lack of air as she fought to hold back tears. Tears for whom she wasn't sure; they might have been for Bart, herself, or the death of a beautiful young bride, but, not wishing to dwell on the subject, she sprang to her feet.

'I need some air.'

Tonight the summer stars were concealed behind heavy clouds that continued to spill rain. She was tempted to return to the warmth of the fire inside or at least get her coat, but instead she sat down on the worn timber of the old porch and hugged her knees to her chest, her mind backtracking over what Bart had revealed.

She wondered what he had been like before his wife's death. Losing someone you loved was a painful ex-

perience and she knew firsthand that when death came
without warning to cheat a young life out of their dreams
it was even more devastating and hard to reconcile. In-
evitably it changed one's outlook and perspective on life,
just as Jenni's death had changed hers.

It had taken a long time for her to come to terms with
her best friend's tragic death and it had also altered her
values and beliefs. How had Kathleen's death affected
Bart? What facets of his personality had been re-
moulded by sorrow at the loss of the woman he loved?

Did it matter? Would it in any way lessen the attraction she felt towards him? Alessandra couldn't help
smiling at the stupidity of her own thoughts. As if anything could! She was totally besotted by the man,
dammit. She seemed to spend every second they were
apart thinking about him and, on the rare occasions when
he'd not been able to avoid her, praying he'd bestow just
one of his heart-melting smiles on her.

In the past she'd been critical of women who were so
obsessed by a man that they'd have sold their soul to
have them, yet she feared she was fast approaching that
point herself. The idea both terrified and delighted her.
Smiling to herself, she acknowledged that conflicting
emotions seemed to be synonymous with her feelings for
Bart Cameron. Whenever she recalled their lovemaking,
which she did at least a dozen times a day and more so
at night, she was consumed by warm sensual bliss, which
turned to fury when she remembered the terse remarks
he'd made only hours later.

She stretched her legs out in front of her as she
slumped more comfortably against the wall. Even if she
could manage to change his opinion of her, how was she
supposed to compete with an exquisitely beautiful ghost
for his heart? Heck, she had never been one to back
away from a fight, but, after seeing the depth of love
Bart still had for Kathleen, Alessandra considered she

probably had more chance of single-handedly ending the war in the Middle East.

'If you've had enough air, I've made some fresh coffee. Interested?'

Bart's voice from the doorway startled her, but she recovered quickly and scrambled to her feet.

'I'm interested.'

'I'm not surprised; it's chilly out here now.' He looked up, searching the sky in all directions. 'No sign of a break.'

'Not yet,' she agreed, standing beside him. 'I...thanks for coming after me, Bart. I know you didn't have to...'

'Didn't I?' he asked, his eyes gazing into hers.

He was inside before the implication of his words hit her. He wanted her, yet didn't want her.

Just because he thought they weren't suited didn't mean it was true. After all, he also assumed her past was littered with cast-off lovers, and that was far from the truth. Alessandra was used to people thinking that because her lifestyle was free and easy so was she, and it never bothered her, but Bart thinking the worst was a different matter. Somehow she was going to have to set the record straight.

He was sitting at the table when she entered the room.

'Ah! Warmth,' she sighed, moving to stand before the fire. 'Sometimes up here it's hard to remember that this is supposed to be the summer.'

'Don't complain until you've experienced a West Texas winter,' Bart said. 'Speaking of which, where are you headed when you leave here?'

Alessandra turned to him. 'I haven't given it much thought. Maybe New Zealand. I'd really like to have a stint at a thoroughbred stud there.' She shoved her hands into the pockets of her jeans. 'But leaving here won't be easy for me,' she said honestly.

'I know what you mean; there's something about this part of the world that kinda gets in your blood and stays there.'

'Maybe it's the people,' Alessandra suggested as Bart's gaze met hers. Lord, but he had the sexiest eyes she'd ever known; just having him look at her was sending her hormones into overdrive. But she knew her feelings for Bart had gone beyond being solely physical. Just when she wasn't sure, but they had, and she sure as hell wasn't giving up on them without a good fight.

'Finish your coffee; we're going.'

His terse words exploded into her thoughts and when she mentally refocused he was already packing up the gear he'd brought.

'But it's still raining.'

'It's easing off,' Bart said.

'Easing off? It's bloody pouring out there!'

'Alessandra...I'm in no mood to argue about this,' he warned.

'Too bad, because I am! There is no way I am going to go out in that!'

'You're going.'

'Pig's bum I am!'

Ignoring her, he began to douse the fire.

'Leave that alone!' she demanded, delivering a heavy thump to his arm.

Bart sprang to his feet and grabbed hold of her forearms, only just managing to stop himself from shaking her.

'Wake up to yourself, Alessandra. We can't stay here.'

'Why not? There's a bed——'

'That's right—there's a bed!' he interrupted roughly. 'And because there is we'd be giving the gossip-mongers a gift-wrapped present if we stayed here.'

'So I'm supposed to risk pneumonia to save your reputation?'

Alessandra heard Bart curse under his breath and pushed her palms against his chest in an effort to free herself.

'It's not my reputation I'm worried about.'

Although he still held her arms the hard grip was turning into a soft massage and the powerful, rapid beat of his heart against her hands was keeping perfect tempo with her own.

'You're worried about me?'

'Don't sound so surprised; I seem to spend most of my time lately worrying about you,' Bart said, his eyes staring into hers.

'Seems to me you spend most of your time avoiding me.'

'That too,' he admitted.

Something drew them closer and Alessandra was forced to tilt her head slightly to maintain eye contact.

'Why?' she asked, moving her hands to his hips, a path of fire burning through her from the touch of his hands on her back. Instinctively she arched into him, feeling his hardness even through the denim they both wore.

'Do you still need an answer?' he muttered through clenched teeth. She shook her head, then rested it against his chest. 'Alessandra?'

'I don't understand why you're fighting this so hard.' Her voice was muffled by his body, but, even to her own ears, her despair was evident.

'At this minute neither do I.'

'You...'

Her words were swallowed by his kiss and the loud pumping of her blood. He held her as close as clothing would allow and nothing penetrated her senses save the taste, feel and scent of him and she held back nothing in her response. Her fingers moved feverishly through his hair as if desperately seeking to stroke every individual strand before her knees gave way, as surely they must, since every bone in her body was at melting-point. A feverish tide was spreading from wherever Bart touched her, radiating into every nerve of her body. When his work-hardened hands slipped beneath her shirt and began stroking the rise of her breast she was sure she would die from willing him to touch her already erect nipples. Her gasp of pleasure when he ceased his teasing and rolled the peaks between his fingers was smothered as again his tongue sought out the·moistness of her mouth. She welcomed his invasion eagerly, alternately accepting his oral caresses with gentle submission and then aggressive response. She would never, never tire of the taste of this man.

Yet she craved more. Her body was echoing her soul's need to feel him more intimately and she stood on tiptoe and nudged herself against his arousal. When Bart tried to end the kiss she gave a hungry groan of resistance.

'Easy, honey... let's slow this dow——'

'It's too slow now!' she insisted, her fingers fumbling with his belt buckle.

Bart was in no condition to argue and quickly assumed the task of removing his clothes, while never taking his eyes off Alessandra as she began to undress with equal haste. The pure perfection of her slightly built body again amazed him, being so at odds with the tough, competent cowhand he knew her to be, but now as she stood naked before him he was incapable of imagining her any other way.

Reverently he kissed the muted pink peaks of her breasts before raining a stream of kisses between them and down over her stomach. When he knelt to continue his task she halted his progress with a shaky hand.

'I swear I'll collapse if you do,' she whispered in a voice weighted with desire. 'I can barely stand now.'

He responded by lifting her body into his arms and holding her pressed tightly against him as he carried her to the bed. He slowly lowered her the length of his body, his eyes darkening as she rubbed against his erectness. Keeping one arm around her waist, he reached for the clean blanket he'd brought and tossed it quickly over the worn mattress. Then he pressed her on to the bed and moved over her.

'Oh, Alessandra,' he sighed. 'I don't seem to have any control where you're concerned.'

'Good,' she said, pulling his face closer. 'Because I suffer the same lack of control when I'm around you.'

There was an urgency in their passion that Alessandra hadn't expected and found exciting. The possessiveness of Bart's touch thrilled her blood and when he removed his hand from between her thighs to replace it with his kisses she was helpless to prevent her cries of carnal encouragement. The waves of ecstasy he created were washing over her with such intensity that she was certain her mind would explode. 'Bart... I can't... Barrrrt!' And it did... in a magical mixture of music and stars that came through her body in shuddering spasms.

She opened her eyes and immediately met his.

'Wow,' she whispered.

He lifted her hand to his lips, but when he ran his tongue over her scratched palms he pulled a face.

'I forgot we smeared them with antiseptic cream. It tastes awful.'

She pulled him closer until his mouth was only a breath away from hers.

'Kiss me and I promise it'll taste good.'

His groan of desire inspired her confidence and, slipping her right hand between them, she stroked him in rhythm with their thrusting tongues. Her fingers danced sensually over his muscled shoulders and down his back, revelling in the feel of his heated naked skin, stilling only when Bart's mouth planted kisses down her neck before coming to rest on and suckle her breasts.

Arching against him, she was dimly aware that once again her mind was being overpowered by her body.

Just as she was about to demand his entry she felt his firmness deep inside; the unspoken words translated themselves to a moan of sheer pleasure.

He was chanting her name as they absorbed each other's release.

She awoke to find him smiling and she knew immediately that waking alongside him every day for the rest of her life was the only thing she would ever want.

'You don't,' Bart said as he dropped a kiss on her nose.

'I don't what?'

'Talk in your sleep.'

'You lay there the whole time watching me just to see if I talk in my sleep?'

'No. Because I couldn't take my eyes off you.'

His mouth was warm and gentle against hers, but too quickly she felt him break the union. Muttering a protest, Alessandra snaked an arm around his neck, but although his smile indicated he wanted to take things further he was shaking his head.

'The rain stopped about a half-hour ago; we'd better get going.'

'You're kidding! It's——' Alessandra glanced at her watch '—ten-fifteen!'

'We'll be there by midnight. Twelve-thirty at the latest.'

'Oh, I don't know,' she teased, rolling herself on to him and nuzzling his furred chest. 'I think we should aim for making breakfast... at the earliest.'

'Alessan...dra, no. We have to leave.' His words were saying one thing, his body telling her something else.

'Why? It's not as if Lisa is by herself. Marilyn's there.'

'Precisely. I can do without Marilyn's speculative glances and heavy-handed attempts at matchmaking.'

'Don't be an idiot, Marilyn isn't the matchmaker type. She's too liberated.'

'Not where I'm concerned,' Bart stated, rolling from the bed and gathering his clothes.

'You're paranoid,' Alessandra told him.

'Maybe, but being paranoid doesn't necessarily mean they're *not* out to get you! There's nothing my big sister would like better than to see me married again. Well, she can count me out. God help my nephews when she starts lining up potential spouses for them.'

When Alessandra emerged from the cabin, Bart already had the horses saddled. Although she had silently willed a return of the storm the whole time she was dressing, a glance at the star-littered sky told her such wishing had been in vain.

Watching Bart adjust the saddle-bags, she wondered where this latest interlude would leave their relationship. After the first time they'd made love she'd naturally assumed they would continue as lovers, but Bart had been determined to keep as much distance as possible between them and instead they had endured a sort of cold war. As much as he denounced any interest in having an affair with her, he'd now revealed he was equally opposed to marriage. So where did that leave them? Bart was already astride his horse, but as she moved to mount Pewter his arm stopped her.

'Climb up in front of me.'

His eyes were shadowed by the brim of his hat, so Alessandra was left to wonder at the gentleness she heard in his voice.

'Won't our riding in double raise Marilyn's speculative eyebrows?' she teased, even as a group of butterflies bounced against the walls of her stomach.

'Pewter looks a little lame. Don't you think so?'

She grinned as she looked at the perfectly healthy horse.

'Hard to say, but let's not take any chances.' She raised a hand so he could haul her up on to his horse.

It was just after midnight when they made their way into the yard surrounding the house. Only the exterior lights of the various sheds were on and Bart reined to a halt some fifty yards from the porch. They'd ridden the entire way without speaking a word, but pressed tightly against each other. Each time she'd been about to break the silence Bart had given her a gentle squeeze, as if reading her mind. His touch seemed to implore her not to voice the question she most needed to ask and he least wanted to answer: where did tonight's episode leave them?

She turned her head, bringing her face into contact with the exposed skin at the base of his neck. His masculine scent left her almost dizzy, yet she breathed in deeply, enjoying the sensual high it created within her.

'I'll see to the horses; you scoot up and have a warm shower.'

'The ride's over, uh?'

Her question hung between them, weighted with both hope and regret. Tilting her head, she met his eyes before leaning to accept his kiss.

It was soft and tentative, but also charged with desire, and she lost herself in the taste of him. When Bart finally broke the contact between them, his tiny sigh was music to her soul.

'Goodnight, Alessandra.'

'It could get even better,' she suggested, sliding a finger down his cheek and across his lips.

Strong as the temptation was to take her into the stable and spend the remainder of the night making love to her in the hay, Bart was still too shocked by the sensations this woman ignited within him to trust them. He was unable to recall a time in his adult life when he hadn't been totally in control of his feelings and emotions; now a snowy-haired Australian had somehow infiltrated the core of his very structured life. He couldn't understand why Alessandra should affect him in such a way, because on the surface everything about her was coarse and unfeminine, yet the more he got to know her the more potent her appeal became. He closed his eyes to block out her partly opened lips and her desire-filled eyes, so he could muster his defences.

'Hop down, Alessandra. I'll see you tomorrow.'

Sighing loudly, she did as he said.

CHAPTER SEVEN

'WAKEY, wakey!'

A vaguely familiar voice and the aromatic smell of tea disturbed the remants of Alessandra's slumber. After blinking several times her eyes adjusted to the bright morning sunshine then focused on the reed-slim figure of a brunette holding a breakfast tray.

'Marilyn!' Alessandra exclaimed, levering herself into a sitting position.

'Well, I must say you look well enough,' Marilyn said, subjecting the younger woman to a thorough appraisal before placing the tray on the night table.

'Judging by the breakfast-in-bed treatment, I gather you expected to find me at death's door.'

'Anyone stupid enough to ride for nearly two hours in pouring rain, at night, deserves to be there,' Marilyn chided, handing a steaming cup of tea to Alessandra, then pouring one for herself.

'It was only drizzling when we left the cabin.'

'You should have stayed the night up there.'

'Bart wanted to come home,' Alessandra said with a shrug. 'He's the boss around here.'

'Hmm. So tell me, how's the bookkeeping job?'

'OK. There wasn't much to do, so I talked Bart into letting me work as a hand as well. Which I'd rather do any day.'

Alessandra couldn't suppress a smile as Marilyn again gave her a very thorough visual appraisal.

'How do you find my brother?'

Alessandra commanded her face to blankness.

'I usually ask Jim. He always knows where he is.'

'I mean, how do you get on with my brother?'

'Oh. OK. He's a fair sort of guy to work for.' Alessandra struggled to keep a smile off her face. Marilyn's expression registered the woman's frustration at the less than revealing answers she was getting to her very obvious questions.

'Are you being deliberately dense or am I being too subtle?' Marilyn asked with suspicion.

'You—subtle? Come on, Marilyn, neither of us knows the meaning of the word.'

'True. Which means you're either being deliberately evasive or else ...'

'Or else you're being too nosy. Now thanks for the tea, but I've got to get to work.'

'No you don't. Your "boss" said you could have the day off,' Marilyn said smugly.

Alessandra swore.

'Damn him. The guys will think I'm getting special treatment because I'm a woman!'

'Gee, you mean he doesn't give *all* his employees a day off just 'cause they were an itsy bit late going to bed?' Marilyn asked in an awed voice.

Alessandra sent her a withering look. For someone who didn't want to arouse his sister's imagination, Bart had sure done a good job of it. Personally, she couldn't care who knew about her and Bart; in fact she would have liked a confidante to talk out the feelings and doubts she was experiencing. If the man concerned was anyone but Bart Cameron she would have poured her heart out to Marilyn.

'You want to talk about it?' Marilyn questioned.

'Talk about what?'

'Whatever is causing that frown you're wearing.'

Alessandra smiled automatically. 'What frown?'

Bart watched her stride purposefully across the yard towards him. Leaning against the entrance of the machinery shed, he felt enormous pleasure in watching the fluid movement of her denim-encased legs, although it was a view he enjoyed even more when he was walking behind her. He could tell she was angry and knew when she was close enough he would see that anger reflected in the bright peacock-blue of her eyes. It dawned on him this would be the first time since they'd been at the cabin five days ago that they'd been together without the presence of someone else. He didn't want to ruin the moment with anger.

'I've got a bone to pick with you,' Alessandra announced when she was within twelve feet of him.

'Oh? Sounds more as if you want to break a bone... specifically one of mine.'

'Don't tempt me. What's the big idea of assigning me to "light duties", uh?'

Bart sent her a puzzled look. 'Come again?'

'Ever since last Monday Jim has been giving me unimportant menial tasks to perform.'

'There's no such thing as an unimportant chore on a spread this size, Alessandra.'

'Oh, really? I suppose checking the radiators and tyres on all the station vehicles is so vitally important it requires one of your best stockmen to spend an entire day doing it,' she challenged.

'You mean *Jim* was checking the trucks?' he asked in a pseudo-shocked tone.

'I mean me! As you well know. How come I'm suddenly stuck doing make-believe chores around the sheds instead of being out with the cattle or riding fences?'

Bart reached for her hands and looked at one side then the other.

'They're fine!' she said more defensively than was necessary as she tried to ignore the warmth his touch brought to her body.

When Bart didn't release his hold on her hands she gave a half-hearted tug to free them. They stayed firmly in the possession of strong masculine fingers. Then his thumbs began a slow rhythmic stroking against her wrists. It fired her blood and as her pulse bounced quicker beneath his touch Bart pulled her to him.

'You're evading my question,' she whispered, touching her tongue to the cord of his neck.

'True.'

His mouth was erotically sweet after days of abstinence and nights spent remembering the feel of his flesh against her own. Leaning into the hardness of his body, Alessandra gave herself up to the pure pleasure he created within her. Being this close to him was both the best and worst thing she could imagine. The best because for days she'd wondered how long she would have to wait to experience the excitement of his touch, and the worst because she knew that they were expected inside at dinner and could take things no further.

Bart groaned as he placed his hands on either side of her face and drew his mouth away from hers.

'I've been dying to do that for days,' he confessed, brushing his thumbs over her cheekbones.

'Really? It never entered my mind.'

'Liar.' He slipped his arm across her shoulders and led her out of the shed, checking his stride to match her shorter one.

'So are you going to explain why I'm suddenly receiving the kid-glove treatment?' she persisted.

'Look, I just thought you might prefer to have more spare time now Marilyn's here. You and she seem pretty friendly and I figured you'd want to spend time with her.'

'That's the only reason?'

'That and the fact I wanted to give your hands time to heal properly. Don't say a word,' he cautioned her when she would have spoken. 'I'll have a talk with Jim and tell him it's business as usual. OK?' Alessandra nodded and the dazzling smile of thanks she gave him caused his heart to skip. God, but this woman was dynamite on his libido. 'Just remember, wear your gloves at all times and stop trying to prove you're as tough as the men. Their egos are taking a helluva battering!'

Alessandra looked up, laughing, but the look in his eyes caused her breath to catch. For several moments they stood separated by mere inches and an unidentifiable emotion.

'If I didn't know that Marilyn was probably watching from the kitchen, I'd carry you back to that shed and make love to you until neither of us could think straight.'

'If you weren't so paranoid about your sister, Bart Cameron, you could be a lot of fun!'

Alessandra eased into a lazy backstroke with her gaze set firmly on the endless blue sky. By rights she should be back at the house helping Marilyn and Lisa with the preparations for the party they'd talked Bart into throwing, but she didn't trust herself not to pick an argument with the older woman. She was sure Bart's terse, withdrawn attitude of the last few days stemmed directly from a series of Marilyn's supposedly innocuous innuendoes about his relationship with Alessandra. You didn't have to be a genius to work out Bart wasn't pleased that his sister had noticed the attraction between them.

Actually, Alessandra was more angered by Bart's apparent embarrassment at being attracted to her in the first place. That was the bottom line in the situation; Bart was ashamed of his feelings for her!

Oh, she was perfectly adequate for a quick roll in the hay, as long as no one knew about it. Ooooooh! She was so mad that she could spit! Switching to a rapid freestyle, she swam back to the bank and dried herself off.

She was still furious when she got back to the house.

'Bart Cameron is a complete and total drongo! I owe you an apology, Marilyn.' Alessandra stormed into the kitchen and pulled a beer from the refrigerator.

'Hey, don't apologise to me. I've called him a lot worse ... I think.'

'I'm not apologising for calling him a drongo. I'm apologising for blaming you for his drongo-like behaviour.'

'Well, I'm glad we cleared that up,' Marilyn said vaguely.

'What's Dad done this time?' Lisa asked, her expression showing she was somewhat taken back by Alessandra's outburst.

'Done?' Alessandra considered the question and then whether or not it was wise to discuss the ... relationship, for want of a better word, between herself and Bart in front of his daughter.

'I'm not dumb, Alessandra,' Lisa said. 'I know you're a bit ... thingy about Dad.'

' "Thingy"? My dear child,' Alessandra said theatrically, 'I have the *hots* for your father in the worst way possible. Damn him to hell.'

'The hots? For Dad? But he's so *old*!'

'He is not!' Alessandra burst out, then, realising Marilyn was laughing, added, 'But he is a drongo.'

'Forgive me my naïveté, Alessandra, but what on earth is a "drongo"?' Marilyn queried as she dropped pieces of celery into a bowl of iced water to make them curl.

'Drongo is Australian slang for an idiot or a jerk or——'

'We get the picture. Lisa, finish off the salads; I think Alessandra needs some sisterly advice,' Marilyn said, motioning Alessandra upstairs.

'You're not my sister, you're Bart's sister,' Alessandra reminded her.

'Yes, but I have never been one to waste time talking to walls and other inanimate objects.'

Once in her room Alessandra sprawled across her bed while Marilyn seated herself on the chair in front of the dressing-table. For several minutes neither woman spoke,

Alessandra pretending a deep interest in the design of the beer can she held and Marilyn in the tip of her cigarette.

'Calmer now?' Marilyn asked.

'As calm as someone of my temperament gets.'

'That's half your problem. You're so full-on emotionally all the time, Bart doesn't know if he's coming or going.'

Alessandra grinned. 'Was that pun intended?'

Marilyn returned the smile, shaking her head.

'You are having a physical relationship, then.'

'Ha! We've made love on exactly two occasions; if you call that a relationship, then I guess we're having one. Bart seems determined to view whatever this . . . this attraction is between us as something so totally sordid it will corrupt Lisa and anyone else who learns of it.'

'Ah, so innocent little Lisa is also an obstacle to this romance.'

'Only in Bart's eyes. Lisa isn't a naïve child any more, Marilyn.'

'I know, I've been telling Bart that for years, but he's determined to protect her from the evil outside world,' Marilyn said. 'He also feels duty bound to provide her with everything her mother had as a child, whether she wants it or not.'

Alessandra sighed at the mention of Lisa's mother, and the sound didn't go unheard by Marilyn.

'Don't tell me you see Kathleen as a threat?'

'Of course I see Kathleen as a threat! Well, not so much a threat as the major problem. I'm vain enough to believe I could compete with a flesh-and-blood woman for Bart's interest, but how the flamin' hell do I compete with a ghost?'

'Are you sure you have to?'

Alessandra swung her feet on to the carpet and paced to the window. How much of her feelings should she reveal to Marilyn? As desperately as she needed to open

up to someone, should that someone be Bart's sister? It
occurred to her this was the first time in nearly ten years
that she hadn't felt in control of what was happening,
the first time since Jenni's death that something had actually thrown her off balance. If she'd once stopped to
consider what might cause this to happen, she would
never have guessed a six-foot Texan with bleached-denim
eyes and a lazy smile would be responsible.

'I'm in love with your brother.'

Although silence greeted her admission, Alessandra
felt a strange sense of elation, as though by saying the
words aloud to another human being she had ultimately
stopped lying to herself. She knew she was grinning like
an idiot as she turned to face Marilyn, but she couldn't
help it. The brunette was wearing an equally stupid smile.

'Are you smiling because you're pleased or because
you find the situation funny?' Alessandra asked.

'Because I'm absolutely delighted! But also because I
think you're crazy if you believe that Kathleen's memory
is going to jeopardise what's between you and Bart.'

'Hey, I've heard the way he talks about Kathleen. His
voice goes all soft and gentle, and he seems to slip away
into his memories.' Her own voice assumed a similar
tone as she spoke. Realising this, she gave herself a
mental shake.

'Look, it isn't my place to tell you about Kathleen and
Bart's relationship,' Marilyn said gently. 'But, believe
me, I think you're reading too much into too few words.'

Alessandra wanted to believe that was true, but she
had serious doubts.

'There's more to it than that. Bart can't deal with me
being me. He can't handle the fact I'm prone to drop
the odd swear word or that I like drinking my beer out
of the can. He's mortified by the fact that I think Lisa
should be allowed to make her own decision regarding
college and . . . and he's got the idea that I've spent most
of my time during the last nine years horizontal. Heck,

if I'd had as many affairs as he makes out I wouldn't
he able to walk!'

Marilyn was laughing so hard that tears were rolling
down her cheeks.

'Thanks for taking this so seriously, Marilyn. You've
been a big help!'

'I'm ... I'm sorry, but it's just that you really are the
exact opposite to Kathleen and every other woman Bart's
ever known!'

'Is that supposed to cheer me up?'

'No, but it might shake him up a little if you stepped
out of the role he expects to see you in and into one he
doesn't.'

Alessandra stared hard at Marilyn and then repeated
the other woman's words. Finally she shook her head
and shrugged.

'You've lost me. I've no idea what you're talking
about, Marilyn. Nor am I sure I want to know. Marilyn,
why are you rooting through my wardrobe ... ?'

'Don't you have any sexy little cocktail numbers?'
Marilyn's voice was shocked.

'Marilyn, I travel light; I haven't room for a sexy little
cocktail number.'

'But what do you do when you need one?'

'Until now I have never needed one. As a matter of
fact I can't see why I need one now.'

'Trust me—you do! Come on, we've got to make a
rushed trip to town.'

Alessandra was grabbed by the wrist and pulled.
Honestly, the woman was insane—they barely had time
to get into town and back before the guests started to
arrive—but, well intentioned though Marilyn might be,
Alessandra wasn't going to be railroaded. As they
reached the door she clutched at the door-jamb.

'Stop!' Realising she had shouted, she dropped her
voice before continuing.

'Marilyn, I'm sorry, but I'm not about to let you drag me off so that I can buy a dress I'll never wear again and in all likelihood will hate anyway. I'm not sexy little cocktail dresses any more than I'm ribbons and lace. I know what I like and I know what I'm comfortable wearing. I promise that if you want me dressed up tonight I can swing it, but I'm not about to spend a fortune to do it, OK?'

'I never intended to hurt your——'

'Oh, for God's sake, Marilyn, you haven't hurt my feelings! If you want sexy I can give you sexy without making a trip all the way to town to do it.'

'You do have a dress you can wear, then?'

'Well, not exactly a dress...'

Bart ran a finger around the inside of his collar in an effort to ease the discomfort and noticed at least half a dozen other males in the room doing the same thing. Apparently he wasn't the only one who would have preferred something less formal. He heard someone calling his name and, turning, saw Doug and Rachel Shaffer approaching, the latter dressed more suitably for a night at the opera and the former in a smart suit like himself.

'Bart, this is so much more fun than a barbecue,' Rachel gushed as Bart shook hands with her husband. 'The tables look superb. Who are the caterers?'

'My sister, Marilyn, with the assistance of Lisa and Alessandra.' He noted her surprised look. 'They'll be pleased to know they have your seal of approval, Rachel——'

'My God! She's not wearing any shoes!'

Both Bart's and Doug Shaffer's heads followed Rachel's shocked utterance.

'Everyone should look that good bare-footed,' Doug said.

Bart was incapable of response. His voice was frozen even as his blood rose to almost boiling-point. Across the room Alessandra stood speaking to Lisa, completely unaware she had drawn the attention of everyone in the room.

She was wearing a midnight-blue sarong splashed with a random gold design. It was caught at her neck and left a tempting expanse of honey-toned shoulders bare while concealing everything else all the way to her ankles, both of which bore fine gold chains. As Rachel had observed, her feet were indeed bare. Bart brought his attention back to her face and felt a pinch of jealousy at her animation as Lisa introduced her boyfriend. Bart had reluctantly agreed to the boy coming, figuring that, if he stopped objecting so strongly to the relationship, then perhaps Lisa might find dating the boy less of a challenge. That, however, didn't mean Todd could monopolise Alessandra. Excusing himself from the Shaffers, he started towards Alessandra.

Alessandra tried to concentrate on what Lisa and Todd were telling her, but the truth was Bart had lobbed into her peripheral vision and her mind was busy counting down the seconds until he was at her side. Four... three... two...

'Hello, Alessandra... Todd.'

Alessandra smiled while a nervous Todd babbled a suitably polite but stilted greeting before allowing himself to be literally dragged away by Lisa on the pretence of getting a drink.

'You look different out of jeans,' Bart said, letting his eyes warm her with their slow appraisal.

'You've seen me out of my jeans on more than one occasion.'

'Yes, but not in the company of other people.'

'Which way do you prefer? With or without company?'

The glint in his eyes told her she was being dangerously provocative, but he pretended to give great consideration to his answer.

'Dance with me while I think about it.'

She shook her head and smiled.

'No way. As far as I'm concerned the only people who could enjoy dancing to country and western music must be manic depressives.'

'Bite your tongue!'

'I'd rather bite yours.' She grinned.

Bart shoved his hands into his coat pocket; it was the only way he could think of to keep them from reaching out and gliding across the delicate curve of her shoulders. Again he ran his eyes over the length of her and unconsciously gave a loud groan, drawing the attention of several people standing near by.

Embarrassed, Alessandra blushed. 'Bart! You have everyone staring.'

'Me? I could walk across the room on my hands and there isn't a man in the room who would draw his eyes away from you. Are you wearing anything under that get-up?' Bart kept his tone low.

'That's for me to know and you to find out...later.'

With that she whirled away in the direction of the kitchen.

Three hours later Alessandra was again making her way to the kitchen, on this occasion laden with several dishes bearing the remnants of the dessert, when she met Marilyn carrying a tray of assorted cheeses. The two of them had worked flat out most of the evening. Lisa, who had promised her assistance, was conspicuous by her absence.

'If you see Lisa anywhere, be sure and thank her for all her help,' Alessandra said facetiously.

'I will. Right after I wring her neck,' Marilyn responded. 'At least this is the last of it. Stay put; I'll be back with refreshments.'

Marilyn arrived back in the kitchen wearing a satisfied grin and carrying a bottle of champagne.

'Let's drink a toast to a successful night. We achieved our objective.'

Alessandra accepted the glass of chilled champagne with a raised eyebrow.

'And what, pray tell, was that?'

'Bart's seen you in a totally different role tonight.'

Alessandra realised that, somewhere between chatting with people she'd never met before and making sure everyone was having enough to eat, she'd forgotten that she had wanted Bart to see her as something other than the unladylike tomboy he perceived her to be. Yet it was only a few short hours ago that she'd draped herself in hand-painted silk, meticulously applied more make-up than she would normally wear, and blow-dried her ridiculously short hair with just that purpose in mind. Catching sight of her pale pink nails, she gave a rueful half-smile; even painted they too were too short to be feminine. And certainly all the women who'd graced Bart's arms on the dance-floor during the last couple of hours had been feminine with a capital F. Of course he'd asked her earlier in the night and she'd stupidly refused because of her aversion to country and western music. Right at this moment, however, if he were to ask her to perform a solo, she'd have been sorely tempted to oblige just to please him.

Marilyn interrupted her musings. 'Thanks for your help tonight. You were great,' the brunette said.

'Ripper. I've finally reached the heady heights of waitressing at private parties. Forgive me if I don't jump up and clap my hands, but I'm ready for bed.'

'Don't be ridiculous; we have the fireworks to go yet. Don't groan; Bart's organised a few of the hands to handle that. All you have to do is sit back and watch.'

As if hearing his name, Bart materialised in the doorway of the kitchen. He had disposed of his tie and jacket and his white shirt was open at the neck. The sight of him, even before he bestowed a lazy smile on them, created a fluttering in the pit of Alessandra's belly.

'And I thought you girls were out here working,' he said, eyeing the bottle on the table amid various plates of left-overs.

'Bart, don't you have anything in your album collection that isn't hard-core Nashville?' Alessandra asked as she popped a cube of cheese into her mouth.

'You don't like it?' Bart's expression indicated she wasn't quite right in the head.

'How could anyone like anything that's so...so *down*? You'd find a more optimistic outlook on life at a convention of manic depressives.' Seeing him torn between the humour of her analogy and what was obviously a strong love of the music in question, Alessandra rushed on. 'I mean, every other song deals with lost love, desertion by a spouse, death or poverty—usually both— and just about any other woeful subject you can think of. Aren't I right, Marilyn?'

The other woman, despite her gleeful grin, held her hands up as if warding off something.

'Pass. I refuse to answer on the grounds that taking sides could be dangerous to my health.'

Bart propped himself against the refrigerator and folded his arms across his chest. An impish look sparked his eyes.

'You're such a coward, Marilyn. Fancy being afraid of your little brother,' Alessandra chided.

'Little? Move closer and have a better look at him,' Marilyn told her, beginning to clear the table.

Alessandra stood to help, but Bart moved, successfully manoeuvring her between himself and the bench. Although he stood a good foot or more from her, she felt the heat from his body warm her. Since his back was to his sister the seduction in his eyes was apparent only to Alessandra.

'Is this close enough?' His voice was bland.

It wasn't and he knew it, but his expression also warned her to be careful of what she said in Marilyn's presence. For a moment she was tempted to call his bluff, since she'd already confessed her obsession with him to Marilyn, but evidently he still wasn't prepared to publicise their relationship. She felt as if she were 'the other woman' in an illicit love-affair, and it made her angry. Shoving him aside was easy, since he'd not expected it.

'Size rarely reflects intellect,' she said and enjoyed his momentarily startled expression.

'Do me a favour——' Marilyn turned to them '—and take this debate outside. With all this dessert around I fear it may degenerate into a pie fight.'

'I'm tempted,' Alessandra told Bart, casting a furtive glance at a plate of lemon meringue. 'So clear out so I can help Marilyn clean up.'

'No need, Alessandra,' Marilyn said. 'Rachel Shaffer is coming in to help.'

Alessandra groaned. 'In that case I'm outta here.'

The night air was pleasant against her bare shoulders and the slate tiles of the patio still retained a hint of the day's earlier heat beneath her feet. Around them several groups were engaged in conversations; from the snippets reaching her ears, she gathered they ranged from rural business to international politics. Everyone was enjoying themselves and eagerly awaiting the night's grand finale, the fireworks display, which was being prepared about fifty metres away. It was in that direction Bart motioned her before looking pointedly at her feet. His face eased into a smile.

'Seems a dang shame someone with such pretty feet would want to keep shoving them in her mouth so much.'

Alessandra gave him a tired look, and remained silent, which made her unexpected kick to his backside all the more effective. She scooted out of his reach while his face was still registering his surprise.

'And it's a dang shame someone with such a cute butt should need to have it kicked so regularly.'

She moved away anticipating good-natured retaliation, but Bart's expression told her he was torn between taking this light-hearted banter further, and the knowledge that doing so would attract attention, thus raising suspicion that their association extended beyond that of employer and employee. Her heart prayed that he would go with his true feelings and damn the consequences. He didn't.

'You're lucky there are so many people about, otherwise——'

'Well, it's a good thing I've got *bad* luck,' she interrupted, feeling the threat of tears. 'Because otherwise I'd have *none*!'

Turning she walked quickly towards the friendly, chatting party-goers, wishing them to hell alongside Bart Cameron.

A fountain of gold and silver burst into the sky and someone again topped up her champagne glass. She'd rather be drinking beer, but switching now would be a mistake; some people might be able to mix their drinks, but from experience Alessandra knew she wasn't one of them. Seated beside the wives and girlfriends of some of the hands, she felt a restlessness she didn't quite understand. It went beyond the fact that her heart was telling her to accept whatever Bart was willing to give under whatever conditions he set, while her pride told her she should have more respect for herself. Glancing across to where Bart sat with Doug Shaffer and some others, she wondered what would hurt less in the long run—selling out her heart or selling out her pride?

When the fireworks finished, the Shaffers and several others started to leave. It was then that Dunc, Jim and another of the hands produced guitars and began playing.

Grateful that she was being spared another chorus delivered in the nasal tones which, to her, typified Bart's favourite music, Alessandra moved her chair to join the small group gathering around the musicians. Sadly, their tastes seemed to run along exactly the same lines as Bart's. She had to admit they all played well; however, despite her efforts to hide her dislike of the music, her feelings must have been evident, because, when the song was finished, Dunc leaned towards her and winked.

'I'm with you, Alessandra, I'd rather play some good ole rock 'n' roll, but the guys won't be in it.'

She decided that the least she could do was help Dunc out. 'Know where I can get another guitar?' she asked.

'You play?'

'Not for years, but I'd like to give it a bash.'

Even as she said the words Dunc was snatching Jim's guitar from him.

'Take a rest and listen to some real music! Here, Alessandra, what'll it be?' he asked, thrusting her the instrument with unconcealed delight.

Alessandra looked to Jim, silently asking if he objected. He didn't and with a gleeful smile she lifted the strap over her head and stood up.

'You can't play rock 'n' roll sitting down.' She laughed at the surprised look on the faces of Bart and Marilyn, then turned to Dunc. 'How about we start with a classic. What about "All Shook Up"?'

Dunc started playing and as Alessandra joined in Bart realised it wouldn't need a musical genius to recognise she was very, very good. Yet another facet to the woman. He wondered how many more there were. There had been a few people engaged in other conversations, but the minute Alessandra added her strong vocals to Dunc's they turned as one.

'Wow, can she belt out a song or what?' Marilyn asked from beside him.

'I take it you didn't know she could sing either?' Bart said rhetorically.

'Sing? My kids have got CDs by artists who are international names and *they* couldn't hold a candle to this girl!'

Judging by the applause when the song ended, everyone agreed. They urged her to do another and Alessandra asked for requests. Although he was aware she'd been drinking champagne, Bart knew that her excitement came from the fact that she was high on adrenalin. Clearly she harboured a great love and talent for playing and singing, so he found it strange that she didn't have a guitar of her own.

It seemed that even the most dedicated country music fans had an affection for twelve-bar blues and pure rock 'n' roll if the various requests being shouted were any indication.

'You probably won't know it, bein' so young, but what about "Reelin' And A Rockin'"', the old Chuck Berry number?' Jim asked.

Alessandra grinned and led into the song. That was followed by 'Memphis Blues', 'Roadhouse Blues' and several Rolling Stones songs. Perspiration was flowing off her as she worked through 'Route 66', one of her favourites, she'd said, when she introduced it.

Dunc had long ago stopped playing, bowing to a superior talent. She was all raw energy, Bart thought, watching as her body moved without conscious effort to the rhythm and her fingers found the chords unerringly. She wasn't just *playing* the instrument, it was as if she made love to it, and Bart envied the guitar her touch.

She reached over and picked up his beer when she finished the song.

'You're really enjoying this, aren't you?' he asked. She nodded and gave him a hundred-watt smile that caused his loins to ignite.

'This next one's for you,' she whispered so that he
alone heard her words, then she moved to a chair and
sat down. Above calls for an encore, Alessandra started
to strum softly.

'One of my idols is a guitarist called Joe Walsh; he
was in a band called the Eagles and they did
this…"Desperado"…'

It was hard to believe that only moments ago the
woman now singing in a hauntingly soft voice had been
belting out rock 'n' roll as everyone tried to sing along
with her. Now their silence was the ultimate tribute to
her.

Bart felt himself swamped with so many different
emotions that he couldn't have put a name to any one
of them. But as the song ended and he met Alessandra's
eyes he knew they all evolved from her.

The kitchen clock was pushing its way towards two a.m.
and the last guests had departed as Marilyn and
Alessandra sat nursing mugs of hot tea. Alessandra
couldn't remember ever having felt so tired and Marilyn's
words told a similar story.

'Well, that's me for the night,' she said, pushing her
chair from the table. 'I'll see you in the morning.'

'It's already morning,' Alessandra corrected her.

'Whatever. God, it'll be good to climb into bed.'

'You're not wrong,' Alessandra agreed. 'I think I could
sleep for a——'

The look on Bart's face as he strode into the kitchen
stopped Alessandra's words dead.

'Do either of you know where Lisa is?'

CHAPTER EIGHT

'IN BED would be a good bet.' Marilyn yawned the reply.

'She's not. Alessandra?'

His tone sent a chill through Alessandra. He was livid, positively furious, as he glared down at her. She shook her head as an image of Todd flashed through it.

'She was with To——'

'I know exactly who she was with! That's what worries me!'

'I saw them when the fireworks started.' Marilyn's voice was feeble.

'Have you seen either of them since?' Bart demanded, but received only a negative response. 'I'm going to check outside.'

He was halfway out of the door as he spoke. Exchanging a worried look with Marilyn, Alessandra hurried after him.

'Wait up! I'll come with you,' she called, wondering how on earth she would be able to stop Bart from strangling Todd if he found him in a compromising position with his daughter.

She was almost running to match Bart's angry stride as he headed towards the stables, and every few feet tiny pebbles dug into her still bare feet. The only illumination against the night was the floodlight on the patio and two smaller lights outside the machinery shed and the garage.

'You check in there.' Bart barked out the order. His tone would have brooked no argument from even the bravest of men, but Alessandra wasn't prepared to take

a chance on being in the machinery shed while Bart was
breaking Todd's jaw in the garage. She stayed with him.

'Calm down, Bart. You're thinking the worst...'

'And you aren't?'

'There could be a lot of explanations...'

'Yeah, and over-active libido heads the list.'

They entered the garage and, flicking a switch, Bart
created light in the previously blackened building. Only
his tense, angry breathing broke the silence; there was
no sign of anyone. Swearing, he pulled open the doors
of the Range Rover and found it empty, so too were
both utilities and Marilyn's station wagon.

Alessandra felt her heart cramp at the worry and
tension displayed on Bart's face. He ran both hands
behind his neck and for a second their eyes met. She
thought she saw a plea of help in them, but he quickly
blinked it away.

'Come on, there's still the stables and the machinery
and maintenance sheds to check.'

Lisa wasn't in any of those places, so Bart decided to
take one of the vehicles and drive around looking.
Placing a hand on his arm, Alessandra stopped him
halfway back to the garage.

'Bart, don't be silly. They could be anywhere. You
could drive till dawn and not find them.'

She felt his muscles tighten and saw his lips thin, his
face contorted in a mixture of anger, frustration and paternal love.

'So what the hell should I do, uh? You tell me!'

'Just wait. She'll come home.'

'When? It's already well after two——'

'Bart! Alessandra!' Marilyn's voice reached them from
the house. 'She's here.'

Alessandra wished Marilyn had been a little more
subtle in delivering the news, which sent Bart sprinting
across to the house. God only knew what he was likely
to do. Hiking her sarong up around her thighs,

Alessandra ran after him as best she could. Even before she reached the house she could hear Bart yelling.

'Where in God's name have you been? Answer me, dammit! Where have you been?'

Lisa was standing in front of the refrigerator looking tired, frightened and, Alessandra thought, a tad tipsy.

'I asked you a question, Lisa! Answer me!'

Marilyn hovered by the sink, looking as if she wanted to intervene, but fearful of doing so.

'Bart, ease off,' Alessandra said. The fury in his face when he swung towards her made her swallow hard. God, if he had that effect on her, she could well imagine how terrified his behaviour was making poor Lisa feel. 'Let's everyone calm down——'

'Stay out of this, Alessandra,' he warned. 'She's my daughter——'

'So quit yelling at her and give her a chance to open her mouth!'

'Why don't I make some coffee——?'

'Stuff the coffee, Marilyn! I want answers, not coffee. Now, Lisa, where the hell were you and what were you doing?'

Alessandra met the younger girl's eyes and silently implored her to answer her father, but Lisa lowered her gaze and began fiddling with her signet ring.

'Well?' Bart prompted in a softer voice which sounded even more threatening than his roaring.

'I was with Todd.'

'Where?'

'We went for a drive.'

'Where?'

'Just . . . around.'

'In other words you were necking?' Bart's inquisition again met with silence and Lisa refused to meet the eyes of anyone in the room.

'Look at me when I'm speaking to you, young lady.'

Lisa obliged, but the look she gave him was insolent and defiant.

'It's none of your business what I was doing!'

In slow motion Alessandra saw Bart's right hand jerk in reaction to the statement.

'Bart, no!' Her words were a strangled plea as for one horrible moment she thought Bart was going to slap the girl; instead he muttered an unintelligible curse and turned away.

'Don't worry, Dad, I won't embarrass you by getting pregnant!'

'Lisa!' Marilyn sent the girl a killing look, but Bart said nothing as he pushed past Alessandra in his haste to leave the room. Alessandra couldn't recall ever having seen anyone look so broken-hearted, yet Lisa wanted to kick him while he was down.

'Still,' she shouted, 'that'd be a good way of avoiding going to college!'

'Shut up, Lisa!' her aunt demanded.

There had been so much pain and despair on Bart's face that Alessandra was torn between running after him and holding him until she had absorbed it all, and the urge to pound the teenager to within an inch of her life for her cruelty.

'You can be a fair dinkum bitch, Lisa! You know that? You talk to her, Marilyn; I'm not sure I can keep my hands off her.'

She knocked gently on the office door.

'Bart, it's me.'

'Go to bed, Alessandra.'

Ignoring the weary instruction, she entered the room and closed the door. He sat behind the desk with his feet propped against the filing-cabinet.

'Another one who can't do as she's told,' he said. 'You want to go for jugular and finish the job off for her?'

'Bart, she's a kid. Kids do and say things without thinking when they're scared.'

'Not long ago you were telling me she *wasn't* a kid any more. Can't you make up your mind or are you just determined to cover her ass regardless of what she does?' His tone was vicious.

'That's not——'

'Not what, Alessandra? Fair? True?'

Again she tried to speak, but he cut her short.

'I'll tell you what it's not! It's not your business! Your lifestyle hardly qualifies you to tell me how I should or shouldn't raise my daughter. And I'll thank you to butt out of my personal life and keep your opinions to yourself!'

He's hurt, she told herself. Like Lisa, he didn't really mean what he was saying.

'Bar——'

'Is that understood? Butt out!'

For the second time that night she felt the threat of tears, but it wasn't because the harshness of his words had hit their mark. It was because of the look of confusion and desolation in his eyes. Being in love stunk! It made a woman want to throw her arms around a man even as he was doing his damnedest to tap dance all over her heart. She should be angry. She wanted to be angry with him, dammit! What had happened to the Alessandra who only weeks ago could have cut a man to pieces with her sharp tongue? It would serve him right if she were to pack her bags and leave right now. It would teach him a lesson. But it would also be the perfect example of a woman cutting out her heart to salve her pride.

'Alessandra, just get the hell outta here.'

'Sure. But just for the record, I didn't come in here to have a go at you. I only wanted to help.' She shrugged and went to the door, adding just as she was about to leave, 'Perhaps you need to listen to Lisa, not a ghost.'

She closed the door and ignored Bart's question from the other side.

'What the hell is that supposed to mean?'

It was Saturday and by right her turn to take the weekend shift, but it was obviously going to be a tradition that no one on Rough Rivers worked the day after a big party. Thank God for tradition, Alessandra thought as she ran once more into the bathroom. How could she have a hangover? She'd only drunk a couple of glasses of champagne. But what else could be causing this dreadful sickness? It must, she decided grimly, have been those couple of mouthfuls of Bart's beer she'd had while singing to stop her throat from drying. Who would have thought that that tiny mixture of the grape and the grain could have such diabolical results? Never again, she muttered, as her stomach finally settled down enough for her to start dressing.

She also vowed never to sing again. The ludicrousness of the idea brought a weak smile to her face; nine years ago she'd thought such a promise would prove something. Last night had signified the final break with her past. It had shown her that just because Jenni was dead it didn't mean she had to give up the thing they'd enjoyed most together. It suddenly struck her that Jenni would have told her she was 'nutso' to go cold turkey on her love of music out of some misguided sense of loyalty.

It was ironic that after years of imagining herself to be totally free the meaning of true emotional liberation should dawn on her while she was heaving her heart out. Jenni would have seen the humour in the situation too.

Alessandra realised that instead of treasuring all the fond memories of a wonderful friendship she'd shelved them and allowed the sad ones to direct her life. After nearly a decade of simply living for the moment and racing aimlessly all over the planet, she acknowledged a need to take root and accept the past. All it had taken was the hot summer sun and a stubborn, displaced Texas cowboy with a sexy smile, a body to match and an appalling taste in music! The thought of Bart prompted recollection of the previous night's drama. She sighed at the prospect of what might lie ahead, trying to ignore her unsettled stomach.

It was mid-morning by the time she reached the kitchen, and even the extra make-up she'd applied couldn't conceal her delicate condition.

'What would you say to bacon and eggs?' Marilyn asked over the top of her cup.

'Something very obscene.'

'Coffee's hot.'

'I think tea is more my line this morning. Anyone else up?'

'Bart's gone off somewhere and Lisa is upstairs packing.'

'Packing?' Surely he hadn't! 'You can't mean he's kicked her out?'

'Relax. I suggested it would do them both some good if they had some time apart,' Marilyn said. 'Lisa is coming to the Great Barrier Reef with me for a holiday.'

Alessandra considered the news.

'How'd you get Bart to agree?'

'It wasn't easy, but at times my brother's common sense triumphs over his need to be in control of every situation.' Marilyn placed her cup aside and clasped her hands on the table. 'As a matter of fact this is the first time I can recall seeing my brother completely in a quandary as to what to do about something.'

'I constantly threw my parents into that state...' Alessandra admitted.

'Then perhaps Bart should talk to your parents. And not about the universal tribulations of raising a teenage daughter.'

Alessandra met her friend's telling look.

'I'm the least of his worries at the moment, Marilyn,' she said. 'And if you're about to suggest I transform myself into the epitome of the perfect little housewife while Lisa's away, forget it. I know you only wanted to help with the idea of me showing Bart that I wasn't all rough edges and no shine, but the thing is, Marilyn...I am. And I'm not going to pretend to be otherwise. Heck, I wouldn't fool anyone after last night!'

Marilyn gave a rueful smile. 'Yes, you weren't exactly Miss Decorum.'

'Marilyn, I didn't come within a bull's roar of being the type of woman Bart admires. But you know what? I was more *me* than I've been in a long, long time, and you can't imagine how good that feels this morning.'

It was stinking hot and sweat was gluing his shirt to his body, but, despite his discomfort, mentally Bart wasn't ready to seek the relief of the air-conditioning back at the house. He continued to ride without any purpose save the need to be alone.

When he'd agreed to Marilyn's proposal to take Lisa to the Great Barrier Reef, he'd told himself that in the circumstances it was the best thing for Lisa. Now, surrounded by peace and nature, he knew his motives had also hinged on selfishness and helplessness. He felt helpless to deal with his relationship with Lisa at the moment. In effect he'd mentally thrown up his hands and given in, wanting to be free of at least one of his problems, and in hindsight he felt guilty that he'd all but filed his daughter into the 'too hard basket', as Alessandra would have said. Alessandra. His loins tensed at the thought of her.

He doubted that any man had ever wanted a woman the way he wanted Alessandra. Unless, of course, the woman in question had been Alessandra. Once more the thought of her with other lovers burned him with jealousy. He wanted her for himself alone and he wanted them to have time alone. It was a selfish sentiment and it had contributed to his decision to allow Lisa to go to the Reef.

Even now he couldn't say whether he had let Lisa go because as a good parent he knew they needed time to think things through, or because he was a bad parent who'd grabbed at the opportunity of being alone in the house with a woman his body needed more than air.

From the kitchen window Alessandra saw him approaching the house, and typically her heart increased its pace as her love of him pedalled it harder. He'd been gone all day, not even returning to say goodbye to Lisa and Marilyn. She'd wanted to have a go at him about that, but Marilyn had warned her against doing so.

'Let him handle things his way,' she'd said. 'You'll find more pleasure in giving him advice, when he asks for it.'

'Has Bart Cameron ever asked for advice in his whole life?' Alessandra doubted it.

'No. But I guarantee you'll be the first one he will ask,' Marilyn had said confidently.

As his footsteps sounded on the porch, Alessandra put two steaks on to a hot skillet and went back to tossing the salad.

'How long before dinner?'

She turned to see him take a beer from the refrigerator, and her action prompted him to reach back and take one out for her.

'The steaks are on.'

'Have I time for a quick shower?'

'You have time for either a beer or a shower, but not both. Unless of course you drink that while you're under the shower,' she replied, moving to turn the steak. Looking back at him, she laughed at the indecision on his face and turned down the heat under the pan.

'Oh! Just hurry up!' she told him and smiled. 'And if yours is burnt don't even think about whingeing.'

'You're an angel.' Bart grinned, already on his way to get cleaned up.

'Right, that's how come I keep tripping over my halo.'

His laughter carrying from the stairs warmed her and she dared to hope that later it might be his body.

Dinner wasn't the strained affair Alessandra expected, but it was awkward. The stress of last night was still tangible, but taking second place to a sexual tension heavy enough to cause choking. Although Bart had told her to stay out of his personal life they both knew that that, given the absence of a third party, was going to be nigh on impossible and totally frustrating!

Since there was only the two of them, she'd set the table in the kitchen, instead of using the dining-room as was the norm. Bart appeared to be enjoying his meal, so Alessandra could only assume that her palate was still suffering the side-effects of the previous night.

'Not hungry?'

She gave a rueful smile and pushed her plate aside, while simultaneously thinking that the man opposite her had the most incredible neck she'd ever seen. *Neck*? Since when had necks been a turn-on for her? Since they supported the head of the man whose smile could melt solid oak!

'I think I'm still paying for mixing my drinks last night. You want some dessert?' Bart shook his head. 'OK, then, I'll fix the coffee,' she said, rising to do so.

'Stay put; I'll get it.'

While Bart went through the mundane task of making coffee, Alessandra watched him in silence, marvelling at every simple move he made.

Each one of them seemed in some way to stir her sexual awareness of him. The way his jeans tightened over his rear as he stood with his weight more heavily on one foot than the other, the way the muscles in his back performed a mini ballet as he lifted the coffee-jar from the top shelf or poured the coffee into the cups, and especially the way his eyes lit up when he turned suddenly and caught her watching him.

Looking away, she struggled to gain at least a speck of control on her desire. She was still fighting a losing battle with her libido when he placed the cup of brown liquid before her.

'Forgetting the unpleasant little domestic scene of this morning, I take it you enjoyed last night,' Bart said, stirring three sugars into his cup.

'Yes, if you don't count the hours I spent rushing back and forth to the kitchen to keep the hungry horde in food.'

'You sure did make an impression.' His broad grin was the brightest she'd seen from him all evening and automatically she felt herself matching it.

'Tactfully you've not indicated whether the impression was good or bad.'

'That depends on whose point of view you want to examine.' He leaned back in his chair and linked his fingers behind his head in a relaxed fashion. 'Rachel seems to reckon running round bare-footed is tantamount to being naked.' He paused pointedly and Alessandra was reminded of his question the night before about what she was wearing under the sarong.

'God knows what she would've had to say about me if she'd seen me doing my Suzi Quatro impersonation,' she said, moving to a less volatile subject and making Bart chuckle.

'Yeah, well, that was the biggest surprise of the night. How come you never said you could play and sing that well?'

'It never came up in conversation.' She shrugged.

'That doesn't explain why a woman with a voice like you've got is cutting cattle rather than records.'

'What you mean is what's a *woman* doing working as an itinerant cowhand?'

'I didn't say that.'

'You didn't have to; it's written all over your face.' She pushed her chair from the table, angry that he had the audacity to sit there looking like the owner of a single-digit IQ. 'You're so bloo... blasted judgemental!'

'I am not!' Bart countered.

'OK, so tell me you think there's nothing wrong with my lifestyle.'

'Alessandra...'

She watched as he mentally tried to compose a response.

'Well?'

'It's not that...'

'Not what, Bart? Spit it out.'

'Fine,' he snapped. 'I will!' he said, manoeuvring her between the wall and his huge masculine bulk. 'I can't for the life of me understand why someone as intelligent and talented as you obviously are is so determined to do nothing worth while with their life! Why are you so hell-bent on treating life as one huge joke and a perpetual holiday? I've seen fence posts with more ambition than you've got!'

Alessandra decided to let him have it with both barrels.

'Because it's *my* life. And because I learnt the hard way that it's possible to kill yourself trying to please other people!'

'Don't dramatise things——'

'I'm not,' Alessandra said calmly. 'My best friend died of a drug overdose when we were in our first year of university, because she couldn't happily live up to the expectations of others.'

Shocked to silence, Bart waited as she took several deep breaths before starting to speak; even so her voice came out soft and shaky.

'All Jenni wanted was to be a singer. All her parents wanted was a doctor in the family, and because Jen was an only child she was elected. For a long time she struggled to both study and scratch out the beginnings of a singing career, but in the end it was too much for her. She said she was tired of trying to keep both her folks and herself happy, so she was shelving her dream for theirs. Eight weeks later she was dead.'

Bart recognised the tell-tale shine of tears in her eyes. Her pain tore at his heart and became his pain.

'It was then I decided that I was going to live my life for me and no one else.' She gave a self-deprecating smile. 'Stupidly I avoided music because I partly blamed Jenni's obsession with it as being the cause of her death. Last night I realised that was silly.' She jutted her chin a little and blinked back tears. 'I'm not unambitious, Bart, just different from most people.'

He swore softly and hauled her into his arms, wanting nothing more than to eradicate the heartbreak from her past, yet knowing he couldn't. Scooping her into his arms, he carried her to the living-room. He lowered his frame on to the sofa, still cradling her, and for several minutes neither of them spoke.

Alessandra rested her head against his shoulder, content to be in the tender confines of his arms, listening to the steady thump of his heart beneath her ear as her fingers drew slow abstract designs on his chest. She wondered how she could be spitting mad with him one moment and full of love for him the next.

'I'm sorry, I forced you into that,' he said.

'Bart, stop taking credit you haven't earned!' she teased. 'No one's ever been able to force me to do something I didn't want to do.'

He gave her a half-smile. 'Still, I feel like an absolute heel.'

'Not to me you don't,' she said, wrapping her arms around him and kissing the base of his throat. 'To me to feel like the most incredibly sexy man I've ever known.'

'Yeah?' He grinned.

'Mmm...now if I could just remember what his name was...'

'Brat!' he said, nuzzling the top of her head.

Alessandra snuggled closer. 'Seriously, Bart, last night finally put Jenni's death into the past. I needed to do that.'

'What about your future?' he asked, unable to stop his fingers from straying to the top button of her blouse.

'My future?'

'Yeah—what are your plans?'

'Reckon I'll buy myself a new guitar.' She smiled as his fingers continued to open her blouse. 'And perhaps—er—make love with you? Not necessarily in that order.'

Her voice was a husky whisper that ignited every nerve-ending in his body.

'I wasn't talking about just the immediate future,' Bart said, lowering his lips to her breast as the last button surrendered to him.

Neither was I, Alessandra thought, but knew Bart wouldn't want to hear those words. Cowardly she compromised.

'I want to be happy,' she sighed as his mouth closed over her.

He lifted his head and held her gaze as he snapped open her jeans.

'I think I can take you way beyond happy,' he said.

Alessandra knew he could.

CHAPTER NINE

'GOOD morning.'

Alessandra opened her eyes and found herself face to face with Bart. It was the most heavenly way she could imagine waking up, just as last night had been the most heavenly way of falling to sleep—wrapped in his arms, contentedly exhausted from the wonder of his lovemaking.

'Gidday,' she said, sure his idiotic grin was being matched by one of her own. She felt herself warm as his eyes caressed her face with lazy thoroughness, and instinctively she snuggled closer. He gave a masculine groan.

'Much as I'd love to continue on where we left off last night——' his eyes darkened at the memory '—I have to get Redskin loaded and over to Shaffer's.'

Alessandra recalled a small rodeo had been organised between the surrounding stations and that Bart had volunteered Redskin as one of the buckjumpers. She slowly ran a finger across his collarbone and smiled as she felt his response to the action against her thigh.

'Then I guess you'd better get a move on,' she told him as she directed her finger down the centre of his chest then made a right-angle turn through a soft tangle of curls to circle his nipple.

'We have to be there in an hour,' he said, his voice ragged. She nodded, moving her hand lower, beneath the sheets.

'It'll take us nearly forty-five minutes to get there,' she observed, closing her hand around the warm stiffness of him. He gasped and in a smooth, easy action rolled on to her and placed his mouth against her ear. A shot of electric sensuality zapped her body.

'Let's risk a speeding ticket,' Bart muttered.

She turned to seize his kiss; his tongue's response was as ravenous and greedy as her own. She arched against him and when he plunged into her her wanton peal of ecstasy bounced off the walls. His release followed almost immediately.

'Sorry,' Bart said some minutes later.

'For what?'

'That must qualify as the quickie to end all quickies.'

She smiled at his dejected words and dropped a kiss on to his cheek.

'It's quality not quantity that counts. I happened to think that a *good* time beats a long time any day!'

As she stood watching Redskin being unloaded Alessandra silently prayed those doing the job would escape the fury of his flying hoofs.

'Honestly, Bart, why you keep that damned animal is beyond me. He doesn't have a pleasant bone in his entire body.'

'He's a hell of a looker, though,' Bart said, equally intent on the scene before them. 'Plus you've got to admire his spirit. I'm going to try and get him used to a saddle in another few months.' Alessandra pushed her hat back and gave him a look that said she considered him loco. 'He's getting used to me,' Bart assured her.

'Yeah, well, there's a saying that familiarity breeds contempt. Let's hope Redskin hasn't heard about it.'

'Oh, I reckon I'm getting kinda good at taming attractive, highly strung creatures,' Bart said smugly. 'Of course, there's a difference between being able to *tame* something and being able to *ride* something.'

Alessandra felt a shudder of excitement slide down her spine. 'Which is?'

'One's pure challenge and the other's pure *pleasure*!'

By mid-morning there was a crowd of about a hundred people. Some gathered around the perimeters of the makeshift arena watching the battle between man and horse, while others thronged under the huge marquee seeking refuge from an already spiteful sun and enjoying steak sandwiches and drinks. Bart had been spirited away by several neighbouring ranchers to look at a newly acquired horse, so Alessandra had secured a prime position on the fence and was enjoying the action of the saddle bronco event. She was cheering quite vocally for a young man whom she'd met once or twice when a cultured voice caused her spine to stiffen.

'I hear Bart's sister has taken Lisa away on vacation.'

Alessandra couldn't stifle a groan at the appearance of Rachel Shaffer, but she determinedly kept her voice civil.

'Yes, she has.'

'So you and Bart have the house to yourselves. That must be... interesting.'

'I doubt it'll make the national news coverage, Rachel,' she told the redhead, who was dressed in immaculate riding breeches and an obviously expensive western shirt, although the woman's appraisal of Alessandra left no doubt that she considered the younger woman's worn jeans and T-shirt left a lot to be desired.

'Do I pass muster, Rachel?'

'At least you're wearing shoes today. Were you deliberately trying to make a spectacle of yourself the other night or is lack of taste the sole reason you were attired like some sort of pagan whore?'

'Actually, Rachel, the pagan whore look is really in,' she said sweetly, 'although I can see you prefer the designer-label, bitchy look yourself. But then it's so *you*.'

The older woman's eyes narrowed and for an instant Alessandra thought she might find herself being shoved under the hoofs of the bucking chestnut only yards away. The sudden interruption of an elegantly dressed blonde

drew the older woman's attention. It was the man on
the blonde's arm who drew Alessandra's.

'Mother, look who I've found. Bart Cameron.'

Alessandra wondered why Bart hadn't been told as a
child that if you became lost you sought a policeman,
not a blonde who looked as if she'd just stepped out of
the latest issue of *Vogue*. That she was Rachel's daughter
was distinguishable only by her chic; apart from that she
looked human. Obviously she took after Doug!

'Hello, Bart, I've just been chatting with...' Rachel,
waved her hand, implying she'd forgotten Alessandra's
name.

'Alessandra,' Bart supplied, struggling with an amused
expression. 'Alessandra, I'd like to introduce Tiffany
Shaffer.'

Tiffany! Typical, thought Alessandra, even her name
is synonymous with million-dollar price tags. Re-
markably Alessandra managed a friendly greeting,
camouflaging the fact she wanted to break every finger
in the blonde's hand that was resting possessively on
Bart's arm.

'Tiffany is here on vacation; she's an interior designer.' Rachel's tone suggested the vocation would ultimately lead to world peace. 'Alessandra is working as
a jillaroo on Bart's property,' she told her daughter.

'Really? I can't say I envy you being in this heat day
in and day out,' Tiffany said with a nice smile.

'Actually, I was employed as a bookkeeper, but I
conned Bart into letting me work with the cattle,'
Alessandra said. 'Bookkeeping is far too boring for my
liking. I prefer being where the action is.'

'It shows,' Rachel said in an aside only Alessandra
could hear, then smoothly manoeuvred herself so that
she effectively cut her from the group. 'Come, Bart,
Tiffany. There's someone I want you both to meet.'

Left to her own devices, Alessandra got herself a Coke
and a hot dog before wandering down to where the com-

petitors were getting ready for the bare-back bronco riding. She spied Jim and a few of the other guys from Rough Rivers.

'Any of you guys draw Redskin?' she asked.

'Nah. You aren't permitted to ride a horse from your own place otherwise it might look rigged.'

'Well, whoever gets him will be hard to beat if they can stay in the saddle long enough to see the time out,' she said, moving to sit on a hay bale. 'He sure can buck.'

'Yeah, him and Goodnight, from the Lane spread, are the hardest workers. Bart pulled Goodnight.'

'Bart's riding?'

'Sure. Why wouldn't he be?'

Alessandra shrugged and gave her attention to her sandwich. Bart hadn't told her he was competing, but then again she'd not seen him since Rachel and the beautiful Tiffany had spirited him away. It was all very well to tell herself she wasn't jealous, but it was another thing to mean it. She was as jealous as hell! It didn't take a genius to work out that Rachel's dislike of her stemmed from the fact that the old witch had earmarked Bart for her daughter. Just how the glamorous Tiffany felt about it, Alessandra couldn't hazard a guess, but if a woman had even an ounce of red blood in her veins she'd be attracted to him.

'I wondered where you'd got to.'

At the sound of Bart's deep drawl her head jerked up. Just the look of his smiling face was enough to send her heart into overdrive. Standing in front of her with his hat pulled low over his eyes and his thumbs hooked into the waistband of his jeans, Bart seemed even more devastatingly handsome than any man she could think of.

'Keep looking at me like that and I might forget where we are and drag you into the hayloft,' he threatened.

If only you would, she thought. If just once you would forget about decorum and who might see us and just go with the flow!

'Like what?' she asked, crossing her eyes and poking out her tongue. 'I always look like this!'

Laughing, he moved her can of drink and sat down beside her. 'So what was it Rachel said that had you looking so murderous this morning?'

'Nothing and everything. Do me a favour and don't mention the old buzzard's name to me.'

'She's not exactly enamoured of you either,' Bart told her, watching her intently. 'You OK? You seem a little pale.' He placed a hand against her forehead and frowned. 'No temperature,' he said, moving his hand in a slow caress down the side of her face; then, realising they could be easily seen, he pulled it away.

'I'm fine. Just tired. It's probably totally unladylike to point this out, but I am suffering from what is commonly called too much bed and not enough sleep.' His sheepish smile delighted her. 'Not that I'm complaining. You're terrific in bed, Mr Cameron.'

He darted a quick look over his shoulder as if trying to gauge whether or not her voice had carried to anyone but him. The imp in her prodded her to tease him further.

'You know what I love best? The way you stroke the inside of——'

'Bart! You're up next!' a voice called from the chutes where the riders mounted the animals before being turned loose into the arena.

Bart's groan was audible only to her.

'If you say another suggestive word the effect you have on me will be obvious to every man, woman and child present. I'll deal with you later,' he said, pulling his hat firmly down on to his head. When he rose to his feet she remained sitting and didn't realise that that was the reason for his disappointed expression.

'Aren't you going to watch?' he asked.

'Only if you promise not to fall off.'

'Me? I won't fall off.'

*   *   *

'"I won't fall off." What is it they say goes before the fall, Bart?'

'You're enjoying this, aren't you?' he accused as he eased himself down on to the sofa.

'Sure, aren't you?' Alessandra laughed, handing him a beer.

When Bart and his mount had parted company, he had already done enough to win the bare-back section, but the pick up riders hadn't been quick enough getting to him and the infamous Goodnight had sent his body head first into the dirt. Although she could laugh about it in retrospect, at the time Alessandra had been filled with cold dread. In the seconds he'd lain motionless on the ground she'd been frozen with fear. In those moments she'd prayed harder than she'd ever prayed in her life. She blinked to rid herself of the image.

'There isn't a bone in my entire body that doesn't ache,' he complained, wincing as if to give credibility to his claim. 'You could at least pretend to be sympathetic.'

'You've had more than enough sympathy for one day. In fact if sympathy was water you'd have drowned,' she mumbled, recalling how Tiffany had fussed over him after the incident. 'What you need now is a hot bath; I'll go upstairs and run you one.'

'By the time I manage to get up there it'll be cold,' Bart muttered as he gingerly rose from the couch to follow her amid a chorus of colourful curses.

'Feeling better?' Alessandra asked when Bart was finally propped up in bed and drinking the coffee she'd brought him.

He merely grunted in response. He was in a mood because she'd refused to bathe him, despite his pleas that he was too sore to do it himself. She suspected he was exaggerating and like all men was milking his injuries for all the sympathy they were worth and then some, yet that hadn't been the reason for her refusal. She knew it

would have been impossible for her to touch him naked
and not react on a sexual level to the intimacy, and tonight sex was something she didn't feel up to either
physically or mentally.

'Considering your condition, it might be best if I slept
in my own room tonight,' she said reasonably, but received an angry look in return. 'You said yourself you
ache all over...'

'I do! But sleeping in the same bed as me doesn't
automatically mean we have to jump on each other's
bones!' Bart said. 'Can't you equate sharing a bed with
anything but sex, Alessandra? Beds are also for *sleeping*,
you know. There's no law that says when you climb into
bed with another person you can't just sleep.'

At first his outburst stunned her, but then it made her
hopping mad.

'I'm well aware of just how multi-functional a bed is,
Bart! Contrary to what you and Rachel Shaffer may
think, I'm not a whore! I hope you ache all night!'

She slammed the door against his call of her name
and was disappointed to see it remained on its hinges.
Through a blur of tears that threatened to become steam
as a result of her white-hot rage, she locked her bedroom
door amid a string of bar-room curses. If she didn't love
him so much she'd hate him!

The bruise on his hip was probably the worst, Bart decided as he gingerly dried himself. Yet it didn't hurt half
as much as the memory of what he'd said to Alessandra
the previous night.

She'd left the house by the time he awoke, which gave
him a chance to work on the apology he owed her,
although even the most well rehearsed and polished
apology would be inadequate in the circumstances.
Instead of simply telling her that he needed her near him,
he'd all but accused her of being a nymphomaniac. Just
because she was the most exciting woman he'd ever made

love with and didn't mean she'd spent her lifetime perfecting the technique. Thinking about her was making him ache in places that had nothing to do with being thrown from a horse. Silently he invoked the Lord's intervention and switched on the computer. There'd be no riding for him for a few days; even sitting in an armchair hurt like hell.

Twilight's last rays were fading from the sky when Alessandra arrived back at the house. She was a hot, sweaty mess and the sight of an unfamiliar car in the yard wasn't welcome. She stood at the foot of the porch steps and sighed before mounting them. She wanted a hot shower, a light meal and three days' solid sleep, not visitors. And particularly not *this* visitor.

'Hi. You look worn out.' Tiffany greeted her in her soft, elegant voice and gave a soft, elegant smile.

While you look like a million dollars, Alessandra thought before returning the woman's smile.

'Yeah, I am.'

'Tiffany brought over a casserole,' Bart said, indicating the microwave. 'We decided to wait for you.'

'You shouldn't have. I'll have to shower and change before I even think about eating. You two might as well start.' To her own ears she thought she sounded perfectly calm, which was remarkable considering she was a seething mass of jealousy. It wouldn't matter how long she stayed under the shower; the crux of the matter was she had nothing in her meagre wardrobe to compete with the raw silk jumpsuit Tiffany wore, and wore so well. She cast a glance at Bart, who was refilling the visitor's wine glass. No one would ever see Tiffany Shaffer swilling beer from a can.

'Is something wrong, Alessandra?' She might have mistaken Bart's tone for concern had he not added, 'Dinner can't wait forever.'

Alessandra wanted to tell him not to wait for her, but to dig in heartily and choke doing it! Instead she was disgusted to hear herself mutter that she'd hurry. In truth she had little enthusiasm for food and even less for spending a night in the company of a man who considered she had the morals of an alley cat and a woman whose glamour and sophistication made her feel like one!

As she expected, the meal was an ordeal. Tiffany and Bart maintained a lively conversation, but, even if her life had depended on it, Alessandra couldn't have recalled what was discussed. She smiled when she thought it appropriate, shook her head when it seemed to be expected of her, and pretended an interest in her food even though each bit threatened to choke her. As soon as she possibly could she pleaded tiredness and excused herself.

Initially the only thing that registered with Alessandra was that she'd fallen asleep in her clothes. Instinctively her eyes sought the small traveller's clock by her bed. Ten-fifteen; she'd been asleep nearly two hours.

'Alessandra.'

Although Bart's voice was soft it startled her; turning towards the door, she was surprised to find him next to her bed.

'Bart? Is something wrong?' she asked, levering herself into a sitting position.

'You were so quiet at dinner and looked a little off colour; I wanted to check you were OK.' His eyes moved slowly over every inch of her face, before he reached a tentative hand to her cheek. A warmth began to radiate from the region of her heart and flow through her.

'I'm fine. Is Tiffany still here?'

He shook his head. 'She left about an hour ago.'

'It . . . it was nice of her to bring dinner over,' she said, then wished the words back. The last thing she wanted was to push Tiffany's virtues to the man she herself loved.

'It was her mother's idea,' Bart told her.

'In that case I'm glad I didn't eat much; my portion was probably heavily laced with rat killer.'

'Rachel has a pleasant side, but it's reserved for the select few,' he assured her.

'Well, you must fall into that category if she's sending the beautiful Tiffany complete with home-cooked meals over to you.'

'You're jealous!' Bart exclaimed.

'Get off the grass! Why should I be jealous of the fact that Bitch-face Shaffer sends you casseroles?' Alessandra said, hoping he wouldn't see beyond her camouflage.

'You're jealous because I spent the afternoon with Tiff——'

'I am not . . .! You *spent the afternoon with her*?' The grin on Bart's face told her she'd been trapped. In desperation she tried to cover the blunder. 'I thought she'd only just arrived before I did . . .'

Bart lurched forward and pinned her against the bedhead. Her startled gasp was ignored as he moved his lips to within an inch of hers. His eyes twinkled with arrogance.

'Admit it; you were jealous of Tiffany.'

She shook her head. 'You conceited bast—'

Her words were cut off with a kiss that ended almost as quickly as it began.

'Admit it, Alessandra.'

'When hell freezes!' Again his mouth claimed hers, this time for longer, but again it was gone too soon and she couldn't help the tiny groan of dismay that came in its absence.

'Tell me the truth. You hated coming home and finding us . . .'

'I didn't . . .' His kiss killed her denial, but instead of trying to stop his tongue's entry to her mouth she opened to it and welcomed it with the warmth of her own. She felt him relax into the kiss and as he did she caught his tongue between her teeth, stilling it, and opened her eyes to watch his reaction. When his gaze met hers she loosened her jaw. 'I was as jealous as all get out,' she admitted.

'There's no need to be. I haven't the slightest interest in Tiffany.'

Alessandra considered his admission and moved to put a little more space between them when she found a few flaws in it.

'Why not? I'd have said she was just your type. Elegant, well educated, non-swearing, super attractive and on top of that she wouldn't be caught dead swilling beer from a can or boozing with cowhands. A lady in every sense of the word.' She paused, pretending an interest in her hands, then lifted her eyes to meet his gaze. 'Just like your wife was and the sort of woman you want Lisa to be.'

She knew her words disturbed Bart. It showed in the way he ran his fingers through his hair and flopped back across the mattress to stare at the ceiling. It would have been easy simply to press herself against the hardness of his chest and the flatness of his belly, and let the awkwardness dissolve in their lovemaking. When they made love there was no past, no present and no future haunting them. It was only them. Yet Alessandra knew she had moved beyond living simply for the moment. She leaned back against the bedhead.

'You're right when you say that Kathleen was a lady.' Bart's voice was clear and exact. 'I'd never met a woman with as much polish and class as Kathleen. She knocked me clear into midfield and it took me a while to hit the ground again.' He paused and looked at Alessandra. 'But I did hit the ground. I admit I loved Kathleen, but it wasn't an adult love or even a deep love. From the now mature distance of thirty-eight I realise we never ever passed the infatuation stage.'

His words stunned her. They were a total contradiction to what she'd imagined. She tried to mentally make sense of what she was hearing, but couldn't, because hope was rushing in and crowding her thinking. She tried to brace herself against it, knowing hope had a way of turning on you and inflicting pain.

'Even before the wedding I had doubts.'

'I...I don't understand. Why did you marry if you...you weren't sure...?' She stopped when Bart frowned and looked as if he expected she would know. 'Well?'

'Kath was pregnant,' he said. 'I thought I told you that up at the shack.'

She shook her head.

'Marilyn and I grew up never knowing our father, and it doesn't matter what people tell you—nothing can compensate for the feeling that your own father never wanted you. I was determined no child of mine would be born illegitimate.'

Alessandra digested what he'd told her. She'd not known the circumstances of his marriage nor the facts surrounding his and Marilyn's upbringing. She felt chilled, imagining the hurt he must have endured growing up.

'It must have been hard. Especially for your mother, being left with two small kids.'

'It was her choice, Alessandra.'

'Pardon?'

'My mother fell in love with a married man and the affair continued right up until my mom died, despite the fact he never acknowledged either Marilyn or myself.'

'Oh, Bart...' Alessandra floundered for words. Coming from a loving, united family and knowing what Bart must have missed out on made her heart weep.

'My uncle was the closest thing Marilyn or I had to a father, and the irony was that he'd harboured an unrequited love for my mother from the moment he met her.'

There was no bitterness in his tone, just acceptance of a sad situation he'd long ago learned to bear. Alessandra felt the sting of tears for the boy who, despite his father's indifference, had grown up to become the finest man she'd ever met. The man she loved.

'He died, a few weeks before Kathleen and I were married and left me his place in Texas,' he continued. 'Kathleen hated it there—the heat, the dust, the isolation—and gradually we came to exist on a level that began with, "Good morning, have a nice day" and ended with, "Goodnight, sleep well".'

Alessandra remained silent, wondering how anyone could have lived as Bart's wife and not been the happiest person on earth.

'Lisa was just a few weeks old when Kathleen died during a severe asthma attack.' He paused, turning overly bright eyes to Alessandra. 'I was miles away checking fences.'

'Oh, Bart, I'm sorry.' The words were inadequate, but then what words wouldn't be? His expression indicated he understood what she wanted to say and couldn't.

'I had to fight like hell to keep custody of Lisa.'

'Yeah, I know. She told me.'

'Sometimes even now I wonder if I did the right thing,' he confessed. 'I mean, I was only twenty, I had next to no money——'

'But you loved her,' Alessandra said earnestly. 'And you were her father; of course you did the right thing.'

'I know...but at times I can still hear Kathleen talking of all the things she wanted Lisa to have and do: a college education, trips abroad, all the things Kath's parents could have provided without relying on the price of beef to do it. I'll never be able to provide Lisa with a tenth of what her mother dreamed of giving her.'

'But back then Kathleen didn't have to take into consideration what Lisa might want. You do.'

'Yeah,' he sighed wearily. 'Tell me, Alessandra, am I wrong to want to give her the best I can? I want her to go to college so she can experience life beyond what she's grown up with and mix with people who can converse on more things than the best time to plant and the price of beef. I want her to see that this world is made up of a whole lot of smaller, different worlds. Then she can decide what one she wants to live in rather than be thrown into a totally foreign one, like Kathleen was, and be unable to cope with it. Is it wrong not to want to see your daughter end up in a marriage that results from passion, but never blossoms into love?'

'No, Bart,' she whispered, moving to take his hand and lie beside him. 'It's not wrong. It's understandable.'

'Then why are you so eager to support Lisa's refusal to go to college?' he asked, his gaze again fixed on the ceiling.

For an instant she was tempted to say that she'd changed her mind and genuinely believed he was right to force Lisa to further her education, but she couldn't go against her own beliefs. Not even to please the man she loved.

'Because being a parent doesn't give you absolute infallibility. Sometimes parents are wrong.'

Bart turned his head to look at her. 'Like Jenni's?'

Alessandra nodded as a lump wedged momentarily in her throat. She closed her eyes and swallowed hard before again meeting his eyes.

'You really think I should back off on her, uh?'

'Yes,' she said. 'Ultimately the only person who really has the right to decide what a person should or shouldn't do is themselves. You can offer advice, but you can't force your ideas on them; people have a right to make their own decisions, even the wrong ones.'

'How come you seem so smart all of a sudden?' he asked gently. 'And don't say it's the lack of nearby competition,' he warned.

'Maybe it's because I've learned that accepting the tragedies of the past puts them into perspective and, once that happens, you have the capacity to seek a future beyond the next twenty-four hours.'

'Come here...' he whispered, pulling her into his arms.

The tenderness of their kiss was on a totally different level from anything they'd shared previously. When their lips parted Alessandra saw that Bart's eyes mirrored the same awe she felt herself. The closest she could come to describing the emotion that made it so subtly different from all the other kisses they'd shared was that its warmth seemed to be generated by *need* rather than want.

'I owe you an apology.' Bart put a finger to her mouth to stop her from speaking. 'I never meant to imply you were a nymphomaniac last night. I was angry because you didn't want to sleep with me.' He shook his head. 'What I mean is I wanted you to——'

'You wanted cuddles not passion,' she said gently.

'Yeah. I don't give a damn how many lovers you've had in the past...'

'Two. I've only had two.' Alessandra held his head between her hands and spoke quickly. 'I've never been one to crawl into bed with a bloke just for the heck of it. Believe me, I'm a real novice in the *femme fatale* stakes.'

'You sure don't come across as being inexperienced!' he drawled.

'Bart, I grew up taping the private conversations of five brothers! I could probably write a book about men's attitudes to sex and manage to sound like an expert,' she explained. 'The bit with the condom was suggested in an article I read.'

'And what about your "I feel positively orgasmic" expression you use at the drop of a hat?'

She groaned and lowered her gaze. 'Until you came along I'd never experienced a climax either. All I knew about orgasms was what I'd read, too,' she confessed. 'I was a classic example of the saying, "Those who can do; those who can't talk about it". And I haven't said, "I feel positively orgasmic" since the first time we made love,' she told him earnestly.

He was smirking like a cat who'd inherited a dairy.

'Well, I wouldn't mind hearing it tonight,' he told her. 'That is,' he added, his eyes alight with gentle teasing, 'if you'll consent to sharing my multi-functional bed.'

'What do you want—cuddles or passion?' she asked.

'Everything,' he said. 'With you, Alessandra, I want everything.'

The next couple of weeks were like a fantasy for Alessandra. She was stirred from her slumber each morning by Bart's whisper-soft touch and brought to full alertness by his erotically beautiful lovemaking. After sharing breakfast they would each leave to pursue whatever chores required their attention that day, when possible making arrangements to meet for lunch.

Alessandra was reasonably certain Jim and the other stockmen must have noticed the changed atmosphere between herself and their boss, but, apart from an occasional oblique wink in her direction, they made no reference to the situation. There were times when she wished she could shout her joy loud enough for the whole of the State to hear, but, even though she knew Bart would hold her heart for all time, he'd made no declarations of his own feelings towards her. For that reason she only allowed the depth of her feelings to reveal themselves through actions, never words.

The sound of the door opening distracted her from the payroll calculations she was working on and she looked up to find Bart entering the small office, wearing a relaxed smile and carrying two cups.

'Coffee break,' he announced, placing a cup near her hand, before sitting in the seat on the other side of the desk.

'If all employers were as generous as you the labour unions would face extinction,' she said, delighted by his unexpected appearance in the middle of the morning. The twinkle in his eyes told her he was recalling her praise of the previous night, when she'd told him he was the most generous lover any woman could wish for, and they both knew she wasn't making reference to material gifts. His unselfishness in their lovemaking constantly thrilled her.

'Lisa called while you were in the shower this morning. She's flying home today...'

The look on his face was impossible to read, and his words hung heavily in the air. Alessandra sipped at her coffee, hoping he would say something to indicate the return of his daughter wasn't going to spell the end of their affair. *Affair*? It wasn't a word that fitted her own views of the loving and passionate relationship which had grown between them in Lisa's absence, but, judging by the uncomfortable expression on his face, that was exactly what Bart considered it to be.

'She sounded excited and eager to get home,' he said. Alessandra knew he was deliberately trying to keep the conversation from touching on their sleeping arrangements from this point onwards. 'She said she has some exciting news. *Good* news.' He gave her a small smile that for a second stopped Alessandra's heart. 'You want to come with me to pick her up? We can——'

'No can do. I have to go into the bank and cash the wages cheque.' She produced a dry smile. 'Ecstatic as you may be by the prodigal's return, I doubt the men will be so overjoyed that they'll forgo being paid.'

'Darn! I forgot about that.' He frowned for a minute, then jumped to his feet as if stunned by his own genius.

'Jim could cash the cheque and then you could do up the wages when we get back from the airport.'

Alessandra shook her head and began stacking the paperwork on the desk.

'Why not?'

She had to admit he'd sounded almost genuinely puzzled by her refusal. OK, perhaps she was misjudging his intentions, but the only way she would know for sure was to ask him.

'Bart, are you going to tell Lisa that we're lovers?'

'Does she have to be told?' Bart evaded, tossing his own question at her and pinning her with his gaze.

'No, we could always just ensure she sees us coming out of the same bedroom tomorrow morning. I'm sure Lisa could work out the implications on her own.' She couldn't keep the sarcasm out of her voice, and the tensing of his jaw told her that the words had irritated him.

'I couldn't do that.'

'Oh, that's right! Poor Lisa might be totally corrupted by finding out her father has a sex life! Heavens, she might start thinking that you're only *human* after all!'

'It's not just her opinion of me that I'm concerned about——'

'Well, don't think you're doing me any favours, because I couldn't give a damn who knows I'm sleeping with you!' Alessandra sprang to her feet and scooped the pile of folders from her desk. Roughly she began stuffing them into the filing-cabinet. Her disappointment manifested itself in anger. 'I'm not ashamed of anything that's happened between us even if you are!'

'I'm not! But I don't want it to continue——'

'Swell! That's all I wanted to know.' She shoved the last folder into the filing-cabinet and slammed the drawer shut. 'Square it any way you want to with Lisa and your

precious conscience, but don't make any apologies on
my behalf!'

'Alessandra——'

'Save your breath, Bart,' she told him, striding to the
door. 'After all, wasn't it one of your country and
western heroes who said you have to know when to walk
away and know when to run?'

Bart had left to fetch Lisa by the time Alessandra returned from the bank, for which Alessandra was grateful.
She didn't want to rehash the argument they'd had this
morning. Not now.

It took her nearly two hours to make up the pay
packets. At four o'clock Jim came to the house to collect
them and distribute them to the hands. Then, since she
had no other pressing chores and couldn't bring herself
to think about preparing a meal, she decided to treat
herself to a bubble bath.

Bart and Lisa wouldn't be back before eight that night
and Alessandra welcomed the time alone, relaxing beneath a warm froth of exotically scented bubbles. She
closed her eyes and commanded herself to put the re-
velations of the day behind her and concentrate on her
future.

Her job finished at the end of next week and one thing
was clear: she'd definitely have to find somewhere to
stay, at least for a few days. The longer she stayed under
the same roof as Bart, the crueller she was being to her
heart. She'd conceitedly believed that by the time Lisa
chose to return Bart would have decided he couldn't live
without her and asked to to stay. She'd never been naïve
enough to hold out hopes that he might propose marriage—he'd made it plain he had no desire ever to marry
again—but she'd willingly have agreed to stay on as his
lover if that was all he offered. Second-best was better
than nothing. Yet when push came to shove that was
exactly what he'd wanted . . . nothing.

She knew she should phone her brother Drew and ask him to let her crash out at his Sydney flat until she got herself another job, but he'd want explanations and right now she wasn't sure she could supply them without bursting into tears. She'd never before had to ask for financial assistance from her family, but then she'd never been in love before, nor faced circumstances preventing her from working for the time she needed to raise the money herself.

The house was in darkness as Bart swung the 4 by 4 to a halt and jumped out at almost the same instant. Behind him he could hear Lisa hurrying to catch up with him.

'Dad, don't blame Alessandra; it wasn't her fault. She hasn't done anything wrong!'

'So you keep saying, but I don't agree,' he said. He was stunned that his voice could sound so controlled even as rage consumed every other emotion in his body.

'There aren't any lights on,' Lisa said. 'She must be asleep. Wait until morning before you speak with her.'

'Lisa, don't tell me what to do where Alessandra is concerned,' he cautioned, reaching to flood the kitchen with light, then turning to look at his daughter. 'Get your bag out of the car and get to bed.'

'But Dad, I just want to say——'

'You've said plenty for one night.'

'Would you pair mind keeping it down to a dull roar? I'm trying to sleep.'

The interruption of Alessandra's voice from the top of the stairs grabbed Bart's attention. He turned and looked up to find her leaning against the banister. She was dressed in a short oversized T-shirt which, as she raised a hand to sleepily ruffle her spiky blonde hair, inched higher, displaying the very top of her thigh. He yearned to view more of what he knew to be the most sensuous body on earth and was momentarily distracted from his anger, but Lisa's hurried words of warning brought it sharply back into focus.

'Alessandra, I'm sorry. I tried to explain it to him, but——'

'Alessandra, I want a word with you in the office.' He didn't wait for a response and marched immediately into the hall. 'Now!'

Still half asleep, Alessandra couldn't imagine what had happened to cause Bart's fury or Lisa's wide-eyed concern. Slowly she walked down the stairs.

'Lisa? What's going on?' The younger girl caught her lip between her teeth. 'Listen, Lisa, any sort of clue would be a big help at this stage,' Alessandra added, hoping to tease at least a smile if not a response from the girl.

'Alessandra, I'm waiting!' Bart's words could only be described as an impatiently furious roar.

Knowing she'd get no more sleep until he'd yelled at her for whatever it was he imagined she'd done, Alessandra turned in the direction of the office. She'd taken only one step when Lisa's panicked whisper reached her.

'He knows I've been taking the Pill and that you went with me to the doctor's.'

Only two words came to Alessandra's mind. Oh, great!

CHAPTER TEN

WALKING down the hallway to the office, Alessandra could well imagine how men on their way to the gallows must feel. Taking a deep breath, she pushed open the door and went in.

'You're really something else, you know that?'

He shot the words at her with the speed of a competitor in the rapid-fire pistol event at the Olympics, then reloaded and fired again.

'Nothing is sacred to you! You just barge on in and do whatever Alessandra MacKellar thinks is right and damn the consequences! Do you *ever* stop to think before you do something? Have you ever once considered that perhaps you don't know everything? That maybe, *just maybe*, there are some things that are none of your damned business?'

His questions were delivered in a menacingly subdued voice tinged with exasperation while he paced back and forth in front of the window. When he paused Alessandra knew some response was expected. She didn't know where to start and it was while she was fumbling for the right words that the wrong ones came out.

'I'm pregnant.'

If she hadn't been so horrified by what she'd said she'd have found Bart's open-mouthed shock laughable. Twice he attempted to speak and couldn't get the words out. Lifting her chin, she forced herself to take control of the ridiculous silence, which was leading nowhere.

'Your reaction is almost identical to what mine was when the doctor told me today.' She watched as he moved in silence to sit in the chair behind the desk.

'Are... are you sure? I mean, you said you were on the Pill...' he stammered, his eyes watching her face.

'I *was* on the Pill,' she insisted, her voice angry. 'I've told you before I'm not a liar.'

'I didn't mean to imply you were,' he said almost gently. His eyes were hazed by confusion and something else; Alessandra couldn't be sure what, but suspected it was shock.

'I haven't decided what I'm going to do yet——'

'What the hell do you mean by that?' he shouted, jumping to his feet and causing Alessandra to take two steps backwards. 'You can forget any ideas of an abor——'

'I would *never* have an abortion! Never! How could you even think——?'

'Sorry.' He came around the desk towards her with his arms outstretched. 'I'm sorry, Alessandra, I wasn't thinking. It's just that when you said you didn't know what to do... I know what to do.' He reached to touch her. 'For a start we'll get married.'

She eluded his grasp, knowing that once they'd been the words she'd dreamed of hearing on his lips. Now even 'I love you' wouldn't be enough. Coming on the heels of her announcement, she would never know if he really meant it.

'No,' she said.

'No? No, you won't marry me?'

She smiled at his disbelief. He sounded as if she'd just told him she could fly. The poor guy was trying to do the right thing again and couldn't accept that she wouldn't fall in with his plans.

'This isn't funny, Alessandra. I'm deadly serious here.'

'I know,' she said gently. 'Look, I never intended to tell you like this. I wanted to sort things out in my head first.' Looking at the carpet, she tried to compose her hyperactive emotions.

'But you *were* going to tell me, weren't you, Alessandra?' His words suggested he had doubts about this.

'Yes!' Her head lifted rapidly. 'I'd never deprive you of the knowledge of your child,' she replied honestly, suddenly feeling weepy. 'Nor Lisa of her half-brother or -sister.' She bit her lip. 'It seems Lisa is destined to find out about our little..."fling" regardless of your best intentions. I'm sorry, Bart.'

As her overworked emotions threatened to get the better of her, she made a dive for the door.

'Alessandra...'

'Please, Bart, let's leave it till morning. I...'

She raced towards the stairs and could hear the sound of Bart's feet hurrying after her, his voice calling her. From the kitchen Lisa called to her to wait, but she ignored her.

'Dad! Leave her alone! She crying! What have you done to her?'

Lisa's voice carried up the stairs, as did Bart's response as Lisa blocked his pursuit.

'I've gotten her pregnant and the stubborn fool refuses to marry me!'

The sun was shining and some sadist was trying to knock her door down with their bare hands.

'Alessandra, it's me, Lisa. Are you awake?'

'I'd have to be dead to sleep through the racket you're making. Hang on till I unlock the door.'

Alessandra got up and opened the door to a wide-smiling teenager.

'Is it true?' she asked, closing the door behind her. 'Am I really getting a kid brother or sister?' Alessandra nodded and lay back on the bed. 'Wow, this is so *great*!' She watched as the pretty youngster's face changed and became more serious. 'But you told Aunt Marilyn and me you were crazy 'bout my dad, so how come he says you won't marry him? Especially now.'

'It's called timing, Lisa,' Alessandra explained. 'Your dad only asked me to marry him after I told him about the baby. For it to have meant anything he'd have had to ask me before he knew I was pregnant. You understand?'

'No,' the girl said, tossing her waist-length plait behind her shoulders and doing her best to give the older woman a superior look. 'Seems to me you're being pretty fussy. I mean, if the man I loved asked me to marry him, I'd be thrilled regardless of when it happened,' Lisa chided, her tone making Alessandra smile.

'You're suffering from over-exposure to Marilyn. You're starting to sound like her,' she said.

'Yeah, well, I bet she'd talk some sense into you.' Lisa pouted.

Alessandra dearly wanted to tell Lisa that she wasn't going to allow Bart to sacrifice himself again as he'd done when he'd discovered that Kathleen was pregnant with Lisa. But she couldn't. She had no idea how much Lisa knew of the circumstances of her parents' marriage or even if the girl had bothered to calculate the date of her birth and the wedding. She might still very much believe that her creation was the result of a great love, and if anyone should tell her otherwise it was Bart and no one else. It was Lisa who broke the silence, which was threatening to become awkward.

'I've decided to go to college,' she said.

'Oh? Your dad will be pleased.'

'Yeah, he was.' She paused. 'At first.'

'What does that mean?'

'I told him I wanted to go to UCLA and he freaked. He started raving about all the weirdos in California and all the dangers to a young girl living away from home.' She sent Alessandra an apologetic look. 'That's when I told him that I'd be extra careful, and besides, I was already taking precautions.'

'Precautions being the Pill, right?'

'He kinda dragged it out of me. I told him you tried to talk me into telling him and that I knew it wasn't a hundred percent safe——'

'Ain't that the truth!'

'But he wouldn't listen. I think he was madder because you knew about it than he was about me actually *taking* it.'

Alessandra was quite sure she was right. Bart's words last night had centered on her interference rather than Lisa's use of contraceptives.

'If it makes you feel any better, I haven't had reason to be glad that I'm taking it yet,' Lisa admitted with a blush. 'I decided Todd wasn't the right guy.'

Alessandra pulled the girl to her and gave her a hug. 'I promise you the right one will arrive when you least expect it and knock your socks off.'

'Like Dad did to you?' Lisa prodded knowingly.

Alessandra sighed and moved away to stand up.

'Yeah, exactly like that.'

'But you don't love him enough to marry him.'

'Lisa, you don't understand!' Alessandra stated. She was frustrated because she couldn't *make* her understand and because she felt she *had* to make her understand. 'It's because I love him too much that I won't marry him.'

Lisa walked to the door. 'You're going to leave, aren't you?' Alessandra nodded. 'When?'

'I'm not sure; I'll have to call my brother first. Probably at the end of the week.'

'I'll miss you,' Lisa said.

Alessandra's vision blurred with tears. 'I'll miss you too, Lisa,' she admitted and watched sadly as the door closed.

* * *

She blinked as she stepped off the veranda into the fiercely bright sun. Walking across the yard from the house, she prayed the tear-induced headache she had would pass quickly. She hadn't been game to take anything for it, not knowing what would and what wouldn't hurt her baby... Bart's baby.

She was surprised to find Jim was still in the stable when she went to saddle Pewter.

'Sorry I'm late, Jim. What am I doing today?' she asked, hoping her eyes weren't as puffy as they felt.

'Dunno, but it ain't riding any of these horses,' Jim told her.

'Excuse me?' His response startled her. Just yesterday he'd told her she had best prepare herself for a long day in the saddle.

'You heard. Much as I'd do almost anything for you, Alessandra, I'm not about to risk my job by goin' against the boss's orders,' he said, not bothering to look at her.

'What orders?'

'You ain't to do no riding.'

'Why the devil not?' Alessandra demanded and forced him to look at her by plucking his hat from his head.

'Durn it all, girl,' he said, snatching back his hat. 'Horse-ridin' ain't good for pregnant women!'

Alessandra felt as if she'd been hit with a bucket of iced water.

'*Bart told you I was pregnant?*'

'Yep.' The cowboy grinned, replacing his hat firmly on his head. 'Pleased as punch he is about it. Always figured he was too smart to let a filly as pretty as you get away.'

'I don't believe this,' she muttered. What gave him the right to broadcast the fact she was pregnant to all and sundry? 'Have you any idea where I might find the loud-mouthed Mr Cameron?'

'Sure do.' Jim chuckled. 'Said he was heading over to the Shaffers' place. Guess he wanted to tell them the good news too!'

Alessandra's feet barely touched the ground as she ran back to the house and took the steps in one huge leap.

'Should you be doing that in your condition?' Lisa asked with a frown.

'I'm barely seven weeks, not seven months. What's Shaffer's phone number?' Lisa shrugged in reply and Alessandra shoved the personal phone book into her hands. 'Find it.'

'Here it is,' Lisa said, reciting the number as Alessandra punched it out on the phone. 'What's up? How come you're so anxious to call——?'

'Hello, Doug? Alessandra here; is Bart there?'

'Gidday, young lady,' Doug greeted her, then, picked up on the urgency in her voice, said, 'Bart's just arrived. I'll put him on.'

In the background she could her Doug telling Bart who wanted him, and Bart's voice was worried when finally he spoke.

'What's the matter, Alessandra? Are you sick?'

'Sick? I'm a lot healthier than you'll be when I get my hands on you! What the hell do you think you're doing, telling Jim I'm pregnant? And that I'm not allowed to ride. The doctor said at this stage I'm perfectly OK to carry on as I have been. I——'

'Well, that's good news, darling...'

Darling? He'd never called her that in private, let alone within earshot of Doug Shaffer and, God forbid, possibly Rachel. As the surprise of the endearment started to fade she realised that Bart was talking to whoever was in the room with him at Shaffer's place. His words drifted through the earpiece to her...

'Alessandra's pregnant and I told Jim not to let her ride; she's calling to tell me the doctor said it was fine...'

'Bart! Bart!' She was shouting into the phone, hoping she was imagining the sound of Doug's hearty congratulations in the background. 'Bart!'

'Yes, honey?'

'Honey? I'll give you honey,' she spat. 'What the devil are you trying to do?'

'Why, nothing. Is something wrong? Hang on, Doug wants to say something to you...'

'No! No, I——'

'Alessandra...' Doug's warm drawl met her ear. 'Congratulations. I must say this is wonderful news. Although I don't know why you don't want to marry Bart; you'll not find a better man.' Alessandra gave a strangled gasp, but Doug appeared not to notice and continued, 'I guess you modern women feel trapped with total commitment, but if ever you want to talk this over with another woman, well, I know my Rachel will be only too happy to listen.'

'Er—yes. Well, thanks for the good wishes, Doug. Would you put Bart back on?'

'Yes, pet?' Bart's amusement was thick in his voice.

'I'll kill you. I swear to God I'll break every bone in your miserable body...'

'I'll see you when I get home, darling. Bye.'

'Bart... Don't——' He hung up in her ear.

She slammed the receiver so hard against the cradle that she snapped off the disconnecting bar. Lisa's eyes went wide with shock before she erupted into giggles.

'Shut up, Lisa! This isn't funny! Your father is going around telling the whole district that I'm pregnant.'

'What are you going to do? You can't very well deny it.'

'I'm going to call my brother and get him to make some arrangements and then I'm taking the first bloody plane outta this place!'

*   *   *

Alessandra tossed the sleeping-bag into the back of the ute and then checked to see she hadn't forgotten anything. Two blankets, plastic groundsheet, a box of tinned supplies, her knapsack with a change of clothes, toiletries and a paperback. That ought to cover it, she thought.

'You're nuts,' Lisa said for what must have been the tenth time in an hour.

'I've been told that by better judges than you, kiddo.' Alessandra smiled and opened the door to slide in behind the wheel.

'What if I need to get in touch with you or something?' Lisa asked, still trying to talk her out of going camping alone without telling anyone where she was heading.

'Lisa, I'll be back the day after tomorrow. Drew said he'd telex the money today; that'll give it time to reach my account in town. Nothing is likely to crop up that's going to require my attention, believe me.'

'Dad'll freak when he gets back and finds you gone.'

'Good. If I don't tell you where I'm going you don't have to lie to him.' She gunned the engine to life and for a moment felt guilty for causing the concerned look in the young brunette's eyes. 'Relax, I've been travelling the world alone for nine years and nothing's happened to me yet.'

'Yeah, but you weren't pregnant by my father then. That alone makes this an act of awesome stupidity!'

Alessandra slid from the cabin of the ute and wiped rivulets of perspiration from her brow. This was where they'd first made love. Memories crowded her head and it was some minutes before her mind could turn away from them.

To her left was the old storage shed that she remembered; beyond that, partly concealed by scrub, was the road. To her north, just over the rocky rise some five

hundred yards away, was the creek. With a sigh she
tugged her shirt free from the waistband of her jeans in
the faint hope she might feel cooler, then turned to lift
the box of supplies from the back of the ute.

She laid the folded blankets across the top of the
twelve-inch-square cardboard carton and placed the
groundsheet on top of the blankets. She mopped her
brow again and blew her fringe away from her face, but,
damp from the heat, it fell back to her forehead and
stuck. Picking up the box, she headed north.

Although tempted to have a swim before going back
for the rest of her things, Alessandra didn't give in to
the deliciously cool temptation until forty-five minutes
later, when everything she needed was unpacked under
a shady tree. Then, after quickly stripping off all her
clothes, she waded into the blissfully refreshing water.

The sun was past its noonday peak and, keeping it
behind her, she eased into a slow, relaxing backstroke.
She was pregnant. She, Alessandra Elizabeth MacKeller
was pregnant! Her laugh burst into the heat-heavy air
with joyful lightness.

Alessandra had just finished dressing and was running
her fingers through her damp hair to restore it to some
semblance of order when the sound of a horse against
the quietness startled her. She turned and saw Bart
watching her from a distance of about ten feet.

The sight of him accelerated her heart's beat. He sat
astride his horse, his hands resting on the pommel of
the saddle. His natural virility never ceased to amaze
her. He was the sexiest damn male she'd ever known.
Her heart hadn't stood a chance since the day she'd arrived and found him grooming his horse.

'How did you find me so fast?' she asked. She'd half
expected him to come after her, but had counted on it
taking him at least until tomorrow to locate her.

'I saw your truck near the old shed on my way back from Doug's. I nearly stopped then, but I figured you wanted to be by yourself. When I got back to the house Lisa told me what you were doing.'

Knowing this conversation had been bound to come sooner or later, she'd crossed her fingers for later, and in a two-horse race she'd backed the loser. She searched his face in an effort to glean some clue as to his mood, to no avail. She watched him dismount, wondering how he could make such a simple action seem so sensually complex. Everything he did seemed designed to send both her heart and libido into overdrive. He also had the knack of pushing her temper to full throttle.

'All through broadcasting my condition to anything with a pulse?' she asked, and was further irritated by his amused smirk and reply.

'You never said you didn't want anyone to know. I figured it was best to head off any gossip before it got distorted. I didn't think it would bother you.'

'It won't.' She didn't quite achieve the nonchalance she'd aimed for and took a breath to steady her voice. 'I'm going to Sydney as soon as I can contact my brother...'

'So Lisa said. And what happens then?' he asked. 'Or don't you think I have a right to know?'

The tight tone of his voice tore at her soul. Oh, God, how she loved him. How she wished his offer of marriage had come from his heart and not his sense of morality.

'Of course you have a right.' She hooked her fingers into the waistband of her jeans, trying to overpower the urge to run and throw her arms around him. 'It's just that I need time to think things through. I need time to sort out about doctors and hospitals and whatever else pregnant women have to do...'

'Don't worry about medical bills,' he said. 'This is my baby too. I intend to support it.'

His eyes narrowed, daring her to argue.

'We can work that out later. Right now all I know is that even though this pregnancy wasn't planned, I want this baby.' She smiled in an effort to stop the burn of threatened tears. 'I'm sure I should apologise or something for complicating your life.' She shrugged. 'But the truth is I'm not sorry about this.'

'You complicated my life long before you told me you were having my baby.'

'You mean between you and Lisa?' She gave him no time to respond. 'I know you think I set a bad example for Lisa, but it was unintentional. And I'm sorry you were angry about my not telling you she was using contraceptives, but I didn't think it was my place. I still don't.'

'I wish she'd felt she could have come to me,' he muttered, staring intently at his hat as he spun it between his hands. 'I feel as if I've let her down, somehow.'

'Get fair dinkum!' Alessandra exclaimed, which brought his head up. She pushed her hair off her forehead and sighed. 'Bart, I don't know any teenage girl who wouldn't feel scared to tell her father she wanted to go on the Pill. Heck, I didn't even tell my mother until I was twenty-two!'

'How old were you when you told your father?'

She bit her lip. 'I've never told him. Even now I think telling him I'm pregnant will be easier.' She closed her eyes as she pictured her father's loving face. 'I know he'll stand by me and love this grandchild just as much as he loved all the others, but——' she faltered as she swallowed back the emotion clogging her throat '—he's going to be so disappointed. I'm his only daughter and he's been saving for my wedding since I started dating.'

'You don't have to deprive him of a wedding, Alessandra,' Bart reminded her.

'I'm not going to marry you,' she stated firmly.

'Why?' he asked, placing his strong hands gently on her shoulders.

His touch sparked flames of tenderness within her which forced her gaze to his face. He was watching her as if expecting to be able to read the answer in her soul. Frightened that he might, Alessandra jerked herself free.

'Tell me why you don't want to marry me,' he insisted.

Trick question, she thought. She *wanted* to marry him more than she wanted to breathe, but she wasn't going to let him marry her for the wrong reasons.

'I won't marry you,' she said quietly, turning away. 'I have my reasons.' She swallowed a sob. 'I can't marry you...'

'Why not?' he pushed.

'Because I...' Oh, blast! she thought, feeling her throat tighten. 'Because I don't believe in marrying someone just because you happen to be having his baby!' she shouted, swinging around to face him.

'So it's not because you're anti-marriage, then?'

His face was devoid of expression and his conversational tone scraped against her tightly wound nerves.

'Of course not! Have I ever said I'm anti-marriage? No. So why assume I am?' she demanded. His casual shrug had her clenching her fists.

'Well, I figured that was why you refused my proposal...'

'Proposal? "I know what to do. We'll get married" isn't what I'd call a proposal, mate!' she told him, poking his chest for emphasis. 'A proposal is, "I love you, please say you'll marry me..."'

'Alessandra, I love you. Please say you'll marry me,' he echoed without missing a beat.

For a fraction of a second the need to believe the pleading look in his eyes was so strong that she nearly said yes, but at the last instant her brain kicked into gear.

'Bart, be serious.'

'I am being serious.' He lowered his lashes, just for an instant, then clear blue eyes again sought hers and there was no denying the desire she saw in them.

The heat of his gaze seemed to melt her capacity for comprehension. His words were sliding in and out of focus in her head. She wanted to believe him, but only yesterday he'd said they were finished. Bart obviously saw the doubt in her face, and she watched, unable to move as his head came nearer. She wanted to tell him to stop, but the memory of how his mouth tasted was causing her lungs to seize and her tongue to fail.

'Maybe I can make it clearer this way...'

His lips were warm and gentle and very, very persuasive. Even as her mind told her that he was simply saying and doing whatever he thought it would take for her to agree to marry him her body ignored it and her arms crept over the solid strength of his shoulders. Wave after wave of love washed over her as his strong hands held her as if he would never let her go.

She wondered how she was going to find the strength to deny herself this man for the rest of her life, because there was no way she could accept what he offered. He didn't really love her and it wouldn't be fair on him. Or on her, living each day in the fear that at some point Bart would again realise he'd made a mistake and regret it. She'd sooner not have him than have him feeling trapped. Knowing this, she still didn't break the kiss; instead she poured every bit of emotion she had into it. She increased the tempo of her tongue and demanded Bart's meet it, she crushed her body against his and then ran her hands feverishly over his back and shoulders. There was nothing about him or the sensations he created in her that Alessandra would not remember for the rest of her life. This final kiss was going to have to last her for the rest of her life.

The push of her hands as she freed herself caught him off guard and she moved out of reach before he could stop her. Tears burned down her cheeks, but because she was fighting so hard just to speak, she didn't have the strength to wipe them away.

'Bart, I...' He took a step towards her. 'Stay there! Pl...please? I know you feel...responsible for what...what's happened. But I also know you...feel that what we shared was...sordid or...or something. I won't marry...you because you feel guilty...or...or because you think it's the ri...right thing to do. It wouldn't work. I couldn't make you happy...'

'You silly little fool!' he said through clenched teeth and reached her in a stride to grasp her shoulders. 'You've made me happier than I ever imagined I could be. And I want to marry you because——'

'Because I'm pregnant...' she insisted shakily, nodding her head by way of contradicting Bart's slowly shaking one. 'You vowed...that...' She paused as tear-induced hiccups forced her to take a deep, calming swallow of air. 'You vowed that if ever you got a woman pregnant you'd marry her.' She looked up to find him watching her intently. 'It's a noble but dumb sentiment, Bart.' She tried to smile and knew it hadn't come off. 'That's not the basis for a good marriage.'

'You're absolutely right,' he agreed. 'It isn't. So I made a new vow—only to propose to the woman I love. If she happens to be pregnant——' his voice had become husky with emotion '—it's an added bonus, not a prerequisite.'

She wanted so badly to believe him, but shadows of uncertainty hovered within her.

'But just yesterday you said you wanted to...to end things between us,' Alessandra stammered, and again Bart shook his head in denial.

'*I love you, Alessandra*,' he insisted, taking her face between his hands. 'How many times do I have to say it before you believe me? Hell's bells, doesn't the fact that I've been boasting to all and sundry that you're having my baby *show* you I'm not ashamed of anything that's happened between us?'

Although Alessandra questioned her own ears, her eyes told her to trust them, because Bart's face was emitting so much love that only an idiot would still have doubts. A smile began winging its way from her heart and she mopped the dampness from her face to give it room to emerge.

'I said I didn't want things to continue... at which point you jumped the gun——' he smiled '—as usual, and wrongly assumed I was bailing out.' He let go of her forearms and hugged her against his chest.

Alessandra felt him place a light kiss on the top of her head, but its effect blazed right through her blood stream as he continued.

'I intended to say that I wanted the relationship to become permanent. I've known for weeks I wasn't going to be able to let you leave. Last night, I was going to have another crack at proposing...'

She lifted her head. 'Last night, all you wanted to do was jump down my throat.'

'I was thrown by Lisa's announcements of going to LA and everything else. I'd only just come to terms with the idea that I had to stop riding shot-gun for her and allow her to take responsibility for her own life, only to discover she'd started without my permission.' He gave a sheepish grin and stroked her cheek. 'It was just like the time I bought her a sweater for her twelfth birthday only to find it was too small. Despite the very obvious fact that she'd begun to blossom into womanhood, I'd continued to think of her as my little girl.'

'Fathers do that,' she told him, wanting to remove the traces of self-doubt she'd heard in his tone. 'Especially good ones,' she assured him, touching his cheek with a hand that trembled with love. Silently she prayed that she could be one fifth as good a mother to their child as Bart would be a father. 'Lisa is a great kid; you've done a wonderful job of raising her. She loves you very much and she knows everything you've done for her has been motivated by that same emotion. She'll be OK.'

'That's what she said after she'd read me the riot act,' Bart said. At her puzzled look he explained, 'She told me I was a prize "drongo" and it served me right that you'd left. She said I had lousy timing and that proposals of marriage shouldn't be made prior to declarations of love.'

His gaze burned with passionate intensity, and the rush of heat through her body almost buckled her legs.

'She . . . certainly . . . said a lot,' Alessandra stuttered, her eyes searching his to see what else Lisa had revealed.

'She sure did. Some of it was real interesting, but I've never put much store in hearsay.'

'What . . . what exactly did she say?' Alessandra asked shyly.

'I wouldn't repeat it unless I knew it to be absolutely true,' he hedged, his eyes dancing in expectation and hope. It was that hope which gave Alessandra the strength to speak.

'Well, if she happened to say that . . . that I love you,' she said boldly, lifting her chin to give her words added clout, 'it's true. I love you with all my heart and soul and——'

He claimed her mouth in a kiss that was pure passion and she clung to him with every bit of strength and emotion she possessed. When they drew apart he was breathing hard and wearing the biggest grin she'd ever seen.

He cradled her face in his hands. 'If you had an inkling of how much I've wanted to hear you say that, you'd beg forgiveness for making me wait so long.'

'A girl has her pride, you know. I didn't think you felt the same way.'

'Why is it that women's intuition never works to the man's advantage?' he asked, swinging her into his arms.

'Why do men bury their feelings so deep it requires an emotional explosion to bring them to the surface?' she countered.

'If they're like me,' he said, stopping beneath the tree where she'd set up camp, 'it's because they're afraid that a woman more beautiful and intelligent than they'd ever dreamed existed will think they're crazy. I was terrified I was reading too much into your actions. I hoped I wasn't, but I couldn't face the possibility of being wrong.'

The insecurity reflected in his words made her ache. He'd been unsure of *her*! She lifted her hand and traced the outline of his mouth, never taking her gaze from his eyes.

'Lisa is right. You are a drongo.' She smiled and kissed his nose. 'You couldn't tell how I felt about you? Considering the way I threw myself at you, it's a miracle I'm not in a full body cast! For a smart man, you can be awfully slow on the uptake, Bart Cameron.'

'Is that a fact?'

She nodded, 'See if you can read the play on this one,' she said cheekily as her fingers moved to release the top button of his shirt.

Desire sparked in his eyes and he lowered her slowly to the ground.

'I'll give it my best shot,' he promised.

The glow from the fire danced over the angles of his face and Alessandra watched mesmerised as she snuggled closer to his naked warmth. They'd decided to stay the night, since she'd packed everything they'd need, although personally she knew that if she never had anything but Bart's love she'd have more than enough.

'We're having a boy you know,' she stated, and saw his scepticism. 'It's true. Don't ask me how I know; I just know.'

He smiled at her and she felt herself drenched in love.

'Is he going to be as spirited as his mother?'

She shrugged his question aside and rolled on to her back to search the stars.

'I just feel *beautiful* knowing you love me. I can't even begin to explain the powerful effect your love has on me.'

He chuckled. 'Oh I think you showed it *very* adequately just a little while ago.'

'No, I mean spiritually and mentally, not physically or sexually. Knowing you love me makes me whole . . . at peace with myself.' She sighed and turned to him. 'I'm not making any sense, am I?' He sat up and placed his arm around her shoulders.

'You're making perfect sense.' He caught her chin between his fingers. 'I know because I feel it too—despite your appalling taste in music and your volatile temper.' He groaned as she elbowed him in objection. 'We might have been raised on opposite sides of the Pacific, but the fact that we found one another regardless proves we were born to be each other's destiny.'

'Bart Cameron! For a cowboy, you sure do turn a mean hand at poetry.' She laughed, throwing herself at him and sending him sprawling on to his back.

'Aw, shucks,' he drawled. 'It ain't nothin'.'

'I love you,' she said simply.

'And you'll marry me?'

She nodded and accepted his hungry kiss joyfully.

'Bart, I know that I'm a bit rough about the edges, but I'll do my best to change——'

'Whoa!' he interrupted. 'Change what?'

'Well, become more ladylike, cut back on my swearing, stop drinking from cans and——'

'And stop taking rubbish and acting like an idiot!' Using his weight, he rolled over, pinning her beneath him. 'Listen to me; I love you just as you are and I don't want you to change one little thing.' He grinned. 'I admit you threw me the first time I saw you drinking beer from a can, but I also found it as sexy as all get out.'

'Really?'

'Really. And as for your occasional cussing, well, it's usually provoked—more often than not by me of late.' He smiled at her nodding affirmation. 'But you provoke some pretty strong language yourself.' He placed his mouth close to her ear and told her what he was going to do to her in very explicit terms.

She felt herself blush all over.

'So what do you think about that?' he asked, sliding his hand along her thigh.

'I think it sounds wonderful.' She grinned. 'Which just goes to show I'm a loose woman, not a lady.'

'On the contrary, honey,' he whispered as his hands skimmed the length of her. 'You are one hundred per cent woman and a fair dinkum lady...'

EPILOGUE

STEPHEN JAMES CAMERON arrived three weeks early, putting his parents through a gruelling nine hours of labour. But as Alessandra watched Bart gently hand the tightly wrapped bundle to Lisa, her heart swelled with love for him and the pain became a dim memory. He'd been there with her through every step of the labour, talking to her, encouraging her and loving her. Then at the last minute he'd asked her if Lisa could be present for the delivery. The request had moved Alessandra to tears, for it had signified his determination to unite them completely as one family.

Lisa too had cried, overwhelmed by the invitation, recognising that Alessandra didn't want her to feel the baby would be a threat to Bart's love for his first-born. Now, watching Lisa cradling her little brother, Alessandra was swamped with a new maternal love for the teenager. It both surprised and delighted her.

When Bart and Alessandra had told her they were getting married, Lisa had decided to postpone college in the US for twelve months. Just yesterday she'd announced she'd changed her mind about going to UCLA and wanted to remain in Australia and attend the University of New England.

Alessandra realised that being surrounded by a whole family was something Lisa had probably craved all her life.

'Forgive the interruption, but how are you feeling, Mrs Cameron?' the midwife asked when she entered the room unexpectedly and found Alessandra being thoroughly kissed by Bart.

Alessandra blushed and reached for Bart's hand.

'Great.'

'Fine. The doctor sees no reason why you and the baby can't go home as long as you take care to bathe those stitches in salt water to help them heal.'

'I'd like to apologise for the way I carried on during the labour,' Alessandra said sheepishly. 'I'm sorry if my swearing and abuse upset you...'

The midwife laughed heartily.

'Mrs Cameron, I've been delivering babies for nearly thirty-five years and, believe me, I've heard worse than anything you said. Natural childbirth is a great leveller for women. It doesn't matter how much money a woman has or how impressive her pedigree is—at some point they all turn the air blue. It made a change to hear it done with a sense of humour!'

'Thank you,' Alessandra said. Then as the woman was about to leave the room she called her back. 'Umm... about the stitches... How long do I have to wait before...?'

'Having sex? Four to six weeks is advis——'

'Not that,' Alessandra interrupted over Lisa's giggles and Bart's gasp. 'How long before I can get back on a horse?'

The rotund midwife gave Bart a stunned look.

'Hey,' he gave a helpless shrug. 'She's my best stockman.'

'Which explains the dozen rodeo refugees waiting outside to see her,' she said drily before once again adopting her brisk tone. 'As for riding, give the stitches a couple of weeks before throwing a leg over.' She walked to the door, then stopped and looked back at Bart. 'And the same goes for you!'

Alessandra burst out laughing at the embarrassment on Bart's face.

'You find that funny, do you?' he asked, and when she nodded, still shaking with laughter, he pulled a hundred-dollar bill from his wallet and waved it.

'Want to bet that you'll be climbing the walls in frustration before I am?'

She pretended to consider the bet, but already his lop-sided grin was melting her insides.

'OK, you win,' she conceded, reaching out to clasp his neck. 'Now kiss me before I die from wanting you.'

'Lady, I love you so much,' he whispered as she dragged his head to hers.

She gave him a radiant smile. 'I know,' she said, but as she opened her mouth to his kiss they both burst out laughing as Lisa's resigned voice carried to their ears.

'Get used to it, Stevie,' she told her baby brother. 'They go on at home like this all the time!'

SLOW BURN
Heather Graham Pozzessere

Faced with the brutal murder of her husband, Spencer Huntington demands answers from the one man who should have them—David Delgado—ex-cop, her husband's former partner and best friend…and her former lover.

Bound by a reluctant partnership, Spencer and David find their loyalties tested by desires they can't deny. Their search for the truth takes them from the glittering world of Miami high society to the dark and dangerous underbelly of the city—while around them swirl the tortured secrets and desperate schemes of a killer driven to commit his final act of violence.

"Suspenseful…Sensual…Captivating…"

Romantic Times (USA)

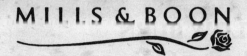

MILLS & BOON

Next Month's Romances

Each month you can choose from a wide variety of romance with Mills & Boon. Below are the new titles to look out for next month.